"You call me a Greek husband."

Arkady crossed the bedroom. "Then I'll be one, Joanna—the master in my own house."

"You'll force me?" She licked dry lips. "I'll scream the place down."

"And nobody will interfere. For however long you stay here you'll be my wife in every sense of the word, and if you don't like the prospect I'll put you on the first plane back to England. The child will remain and we'll manage somehow. Ilone will find a nurse, or I'll..."

The mention of Ilone made Joanna shake with rage. "No, you won't," she spat. "He's *my* baby!" Then her defiance collapsed. "Very well, I'll stay, and we'll play it your way—and a lot of joy you'll get out of it!"

Books by Jeneth Murrey

HARLEQUIN ROMANCE

HARLEQUIN PRESENTS

These books may be available at your local bookseller.

Don't miss any of our special offers. Write to us at the following address for information on our newest releases.

Harlequin Reader Service
P.O. Box 52040, Phoenix, AZ 85072-2040
Canadian address: P.O. Box 2800, Postal Station A,
5170 Yonge St., Willowdale, Ont. M2N6J3

Return to Arkady

Jeneth Murrey

Harlequin Books

TORONTO • NEW YORK • LONDON
AMSTERDAM • PARIS • SYDNEY • HAMBURG
STOCKHOLM • ATHENS • TOKYO • MILAN

Original hardcover edition published in 1985
by Mills & Boon Limited

ISBN 0-373-02728-1

Harlequin Romance first edition November 1985

CHAPTER ONE

OUTSIDE the window, the heavy, dull clouds seemed almost to touch the roofs of the houses and the rain fell steadily—not a good, honest-to-God downpour to streak down the panes, hard, fast and soon over, but a quiet, relentless wetting of everything. Even indoors, the air felt full of moisture and a film of dampness seemed to cling to everything.

Joanna swished the curtains across the living-room window. Although it was only two o'clock in the afternoon, she could bear the dreariness outside no longer—it saddened her, and she dropped on to her knees to light the gas fire. The automatic ignition thing was broken and matches were too short, so she resorted to a paper spill, blowing ferociously until the jet caught with a distinct pop, then she hurried out into the small hallway of her first floor flat to feed coins into the gas meter. On her way back to the living-room, she stopped to look at her reflection in the mirror, standing well back to get an overall inspection.

It had ceased to surprise her that she hardly recognised herself, it was like looking at a stranger—there was very little of the old Joanna left. Her face was hollowed, the skin drawn drum-tight across the bones so that her eyes looked huge and sunken and her straight nose stood out like a beak. The eyes were different as well—still wide-spaced and fringed with long, dark lashes, but their clear, bright grey, without a trace of either blue or green, had darkened and dulled until they looked the same colour as the rain-filled clouds.

The rest of her—she pulled at the waist of her dress, tightening it about her, and shook her head at the reflection. Too thin, the health visitor had said—she should eat more, and she'd done her best, but food seemed to have lost its savour. All the same, she decided, she'd have to try a bit harder. She had always been slender, but now, with her stick-like arms and legs, the way her hip-bones jutted, she looked almost skeletal. There wasn't an ounce of fat on her anywhere, and not so much flesh either.

But it was her hair she mourned most—she had always thought of it as her one truly beautiful feature. The rest of her wasn't too bad, she had once passed for a good-looking young woman, but her hair—falling to well below her shoulders in a straight, silky curtain of rose-gold—she had been proud of it, but not any longer. The light in the hallway was poor, a small-powered bulb high up in the ceiling concealed a lot, but it couldn't hide the fact that her hair had suffered. The rosy gold was now an anonymous tow colour, neither blonde nor brunette, and it was dead-looking, greasy and lank no matter how often she washed it.

'Lifeless and dreary,' she said aloud to shake herself out of her depression. 'But you've got one bright spot in your life, so get to it, my girl,' as a lusty wail came from the bedroom. 'Your bright spot thinks he's slept enough!' She often found she was talking to herself nowadays—a bad sign, that, and she hurried to where her three-month-old son was protesting about being kept waiting for his feed.

As soon as she picked him up from his crib, his cries ceased and he smiled widely at her. 'And that's a real smile,' she told him. 'You didn't cross your eyes that time—and by the way, my lad, you're getting heavy,' she murmured against the black fluff of his hair as she stooped to pick up his toilet basket. 'Don't you dare to grow out of that sleeping suit for a couple more weeks—all right, darling,' as he grew impatient and squared his little mouth for another yell. 'But we have to make you comfy first.'

She felt his well-padded rear and grinned as she hugged him. 'I'll clean you up and you shall have a little kick on the floor by the fire, free of all this nasty plastic, before we get to the staff of your life.'

All the time she was changing him, cleaning him up and sponging his face and hands, she kept up the murmur of nonsense while she watched his face with huge, anxious eyes, searching for the resemblance which she had thought she had seen once or twice, and suddenly it was there, fleetingly. Cloudy blue eyes, so deep a blue they were almost purple, looked up at her as she wiped his face with a towel and black eyebrows quirked into a tiny frown. She had known heaven, but it had been for such a short time before she had been driven out of it and then, when the pain of her loss had been almost too great to be borne, there had been this tiny part of the glory given back to her. The resemblance was gone, as swiftly as it had come, and with a soft sigh, Joanna enveloped the baby in a blanket and carried him into the living-room, where she spread the blanket on the hearthrug and laid him down on it.

Memory came back to taunt her and she was back on the island under the hot sun and the blue, blue sky—sunning herself on the half moon of silky, almost silver sand and looking up at the villa on the headland so far above her—the white walls, the arcaded terrace and the splashes of violent colour from bougainvillaea and oleander which sprawled over everything.

When she had first seen the house, she had thought it was part of paradise, that she couldn't fail to be happy there, but—The click of the door brought her back to the present, the sun, the sea and the scents of rosemary and thyme vanished and her landlady was speaking from the doorway.

'Well, I don't know if I should, sir. Mrs Marr may not want ... Oooh ...' The door clicked again, there was a soft step in the hallway, Joanna felt a slight draught as the living-room door was opened and a well remembered voice—too well remembered—said her name.

'Joanna!'

For a moment she was incapable of movement, frozen into position by something like terror. Her mouth opened, but there were no words, only an animal-like sound compounded of hurt and fright. Her eyes slid down to the baby, lying on the rug, and the sight of him broke the spell that held her still. She launched herself from the chair, grabbed at him, lifting him and hugging him to her bosom. The suddenness of it frightened him and he screamed.

'You're hurting him, Joanna.' The man advanced towards her across the well polished linoleum, his damp shoes making smeary marks on the shiny surface, and at last she found her tongue.

'No,' she shook her head violently. 'No, no, *no*! Go away, go back to where you came from, you're not wanted here!' She tried not to hear the small voice in her mind that told her she *did* want him, that she had never wanted any other man—that no matter how badly he had behaved, she still wanted him and she would go on wanting till the day she died. She fought it grimly until it ceased, while her arms tightened further about her son and her eyes slid from side to side like those of a trapped animal. 'You shan't have him, he's mine!' It came out breathy, shrill and slightly hysterical, but under the hysteria and the breathiness was a grim determination.

'Joanna!' The whiplike tone was as good as cold water thrown in her face, and with a bump she sat down in the chair, smarting under the lash of it but thankful for it in a curious way. It had killed her fright stone dead, stone cold, and the coldness spread right through her so that she could think properly once more. 'Look at me, you little fool! I'm not going to tear the child away from you,' he continued harshly, 'so stop looking at me as though I'm a stranger come to ravish you. I'm your husband, come to see my son and talk sensibly about the future with my wife.'

Slowly Joanna could feel the panic leaving her; whatever other faults he had, Arkady St Vlastos wasn't given to physical violence. Arkady—her mind lingered on the name. Such an unusual name for a Greek—it wasn't a Greek name, only a whim of his American mother, a play on the name she

had given to the house—Arcadia. And he didn't
look like a Greek, he was too tall, too rangy; his
legs were too long and, in profile, his high
cheekbones, hooked nose, deepset, very dark eyes;
the thin mouth which could curve into a smile or
straighten in a hard, uncompromising line and his
long, firm chin were more like the features of an
American Indian—but inside, he was Greek all
through, right to his backbone.

Still, she comforted herself, even if he did get
nasty, she had nothing to fear. He had left the
living-room door open, her landlady lived just
below her, on the ground floor—one good scream
would bring everybody running.

'What future?' She hadn't gained complete
control of herself, her voice still wobbled, but as
soon as her heart stopped beating like a trip-
hammer, she would have that under control. 'Our
future?' That was better, she'd managed to get the
right sarcastic touch. 'We haven't one—you killed
that off over a year ago. My future—oh no! That
hasn't got anything to do with you either, so we
don't have to talk about that . . .'

'My son's future, then.' Arkady's dark eyes were
almost hidden beneath his heavy lids and his mouth
was in the old, familiar straight line. A little nerve
jerked at the corner of his mouth—a bad sign,
that—it meant he was beginning to lose his temper.
In a spirit of defiance, Joanna needled him a bit more.

'*My* son—oh, I don't deny you fathered him,
but apart from that, there's nothing . . .'

'You put my name on the birth certificate,' he
reminded her. 'And what do you mean by calling
yourself Mrs Marr? If you want to be English
about it, you're Mrs St Vlastos.'

'I can call myself what I like,' she lifted her chin, almost enjoying the fight, 'and I choose to be Mrs Marr. I've resigned from the position as your wife. I'm written down on the records as a one-parent family—and now,' she jogged the baby to hush his wailing, *my* son's hungry, he wants to be fed, so I'd be obliged if you'd go. We neither of us appreciate an audience.'

'Then feed him,' he dictated harshly. 'Hell, woman, why all the modesty? We're married, you lived with me for a year and there's not an inch of you I don't know.'

Joanna sat down with her child, but before she unbuttoned the front of her dress, she wriggled a crocheted shawl over her shoulder to make a screen—and nearly jumped out of her skin at his derisive laugh.

'I wish you'd go away, right away,' she muttered desperately.

'I refuse,' and he nodded at the baby, who was gulping greedily. 'You called him Dionysus.'

This was a comparatively safe subject, so she could return his nod serenely. 'He won't love me for doing that, I call him Dion,' and to keep the subject safe, give him no time to start laying down the law, 'How did you find me?'

Arkady passed her to slump into the chair opposite. 'I never lost you, my dear,' and at her raised eyebrows, 'You want a résumé of everything you've done since you left my house—I can provide it. You came straight back to England and for a month, you lived with your aunt in Bedford. When she died you left there, came to London and started working again for your old firm and you lived in a bedsitter . . .'

'You had me watched!' she accused, lifting her chin and looking down her nose in disgust.

'Not necessary,' he shook his head. 'I had made a small investment in the firm. The work it did was good, but the competition from Italy was forcing them into bankruptcy, they desperately needed a fresh injection of capital to buy new presses and machinery . . .'

'And in return,' Joanna said bitterly, 'somebody fed you all the information about me.'

'About all the staff,' he smiled at her mockingly.

'Then why the delay? Why did you wait until now?'

Arkady's eyes hardened. 'You left, just before I had a chance to get to London. You vanished, and I had to be very nice to a private secretary before I could get the information I needed. I was very discreet, the lady was like an oyster when it came to business, but she liked a juicy bit of gossip, especially about her colleagues, and you, my dear, were the subject of a great deal of speculation. She didn't know I was your husband, of course; you didn't tell anybody about our marriage, did you? And the lady wasn't at all sure you *were* married, but of one thing she *was* sure—you were going to have a baby. She said it was obvious to her as soon as you rejoined the firm.'

The firm—Joanna's eyes misted. Her first employers, her only employers—producers of travel brochures—she'd joined them as a photographer straight from school and worked happily for them for four years until she had been sent out to Corfu to photograph a batch of newly built holiday villas, the luxury type. A new holiday company had been formed in Greece; she had had it all explained to her—a company which was aiming for the upper end of the market—a de-luxe villa with maid service and a Cordon Bleu cook; private pool, complete privacy, a hire car, even a motorboat if one was required—and she was to photograph the villas.

It had been quite a feather in her cap, previously her most important assignment had been the photographing of Stately Home interiors for guide-books. The firm was too small to have its own photographer do the foreign work, the hotels and apartment complexes had always supplied their own illustrations—and it was while Joanna had been hard at work in Corfu that she had met Arkady.

A small smile curved her mouth as she remembered that meeting. She had finished the exterior shots of the particular villa and rigged up a couple of arc lamps and a trestle to stand on in one of the bedrooms when he had come in, knocking over a lamp, smashing the bulb and telling her to hurry. She hadn't known who he was, so she hadn't been polite—how *was* she supposed to know it was his holiday villa company which was employing her, nobody had ever mentioned his name and he hadn't looked the part in faded jeans and tee-shirt.

She had stormed at him for messing up her equipment—told him what she thought about the public transport on the island—that hadn't been complimentary either. He had offered her a hire car and she'd snapped his head off, telling him she couldn't drive, and then suggested he get the hell out of the place before he did any more damage! A stormy beginning to a sort of holiday romance—

her mouth tightened; it would have been better if she'd left it at that—a holiday romance, something to be a bit tender about when she returned to England, something to remember with a smile when wet autumn slid into cold winter—dinners at outdoor restaurants, always called The Olive Press—there were so many olive trees in Corfu, it seemed natural; the whole island seemed covered with them so there must have been dozens of presses scattered about. The boat trips he'd taken her on when they'd dived off the side into water so clear she could see the rocky sea bed beneath her. Some kisses, warm and exciting, but he had never asked more than that from her, and she had loved him, cast caution to the winds because of that love, to marry him almost as soon as he had asked her.

He had been quite honest with her—or so she had thought—telling her about his first marriage, that he was a widower with a young daughter; Kore was fifteen, so he said. Telling her as well that he wasn't wealthy, just comfortably off, but that she would never lack for anything she wanted—that all his money was tied up in the new villa company and about the other villas he planned as soon as the ones on Corfu showed a profit.

After their quiet wedding—it had taken place in Athens, and they had spent a week sightseeing; Delphi, the Acropolis, lots of places which Joanna had never heard of and didn't remember much about—she had been too bemused by happiness to pay much attention to where they went or what they saw; they had returned to Arkady's home in Corfu, the Arcadian villa on the headland a few miles north of Paleokastritsa, and there the rot had set in.

Her eyes darkened with painful memories. She could feel tears behind her eyelids and she closed them tight. She still loved Arkady even though she knew now that he wasn't worth her love, but that didn't mean she had to be soft about him.

'So,' she snorted softly, 'having lost me again, what did you do then?'

Arkady laughed softly—as he'd laughed so often in the past when he was teasing her. 'We-ell,' he drew it out aggravatingly as he lit a cigarette, delaying his reply until he'd blown a cloud of smoke up to the ceiling, 'the high-powered secretary, as I said, was short on actual facts, so all I really had from that very expensive dinner was the fact that you were going to have a baby—but you English are very methodical about matters like births, deaths and marriages. All the records complete, gathered together in one place and open to inspection—very neat. And I took a chance you'd conform, not give false information on an official document. I had a firm of solicitors check the records,' and at her gasp of outrage, he shook his head. 'They didn't know what they were doing—not precisely. I told them it was a matter of inheritance. They provided me with a copy of the baby's birth certificate—after that, it was easy. People tend to remember a baby with the unusual name of Dionysus St Vlastos, they remember where his mother took him when they left hospital—but, feeling as you obviously do about me, why did you give him a Greek name?'

The baby had finished feeding and Joanna set him on her knee to rub his back. He burped satisfactorily and she delayed answering while she wiped away the milky dribble from his tiny mouth with a tissue.

'I call him Dion,' she repeated finally, and then, belligerently, 'Dion Marr. Later on, when he's old enough to understand, I shall explain things to him and he can decide for himself which name he'll use.'

'Generous, even if you didn't answer the question.' He was mocking her, and she flushed but let him continue as she fastened the baby's nappy and inserted him into a clean sleeping suit. 'However, there'll be time enough to talk about that later. How soon can you be ready to leave?'

Had she been waiting for just this question? She didn't know, but she thought that, somewhere at the back of her mind, she had been expecting it; it didn't shock her, and as she steered a tiny arm into a sleeve she heard herself being cool and composed.

'A stupid question and you know it. I've no intention of leaving. I'm staying here, this is my home now, mine and Dion's.'

'As you wish.' Arkady sounded indifferent, but his mouth was in the familiar straight line—it had often looked like that during the latter months of what Joanna termed their mistaken marriage. But she wasn't going to be intimidated by a stern, hard expression. He had to be made to realise she was no longer a chattel, an inferior being, because she was a woman. He had to learn that she was capable of thinking and managing for herself.

'*Just* as I wish,' she agreed with him emphatically, and waited for the crunch—Arkady wouldn't take it lying down—and it came, much as she'd expected, but although she was trembling like a leaf inside, she didn't allow her trepidation to show.

'It's your decision,' he said as though he was discussing some business proposition and not as though there were any feelings involved. 'But the boy, my son, comes with me—and I think there's something else you should take into consideration. I've no intention of marrying again—two wives is enough for any man, so there will be no divorce for you.'

It hit her like a hammer blow, his quietness, his implacability, and her voice started to wobble again as she defied him.

'No, you can't have my baby! I'm his mother...'

'It's all you seem able to say, No,' he reproved her, still quiet but with an air of hidden menace. 'But I don't think you have much choice, Joanna—not if you want to be with the child. I shall take him, make no mistake about that, by force if it's necessary—I can have him back in either Greece or Corfu long before you can get a court order to stop me—and if you're thinking about the formalities, I shan't be doing anything illegal. I've a friend from the Embassy standing by with all the necessary documentation. Dion may have been born in England of an English mother, but he's a Greek national. By the way, thank you for being so truthful on my son's birth certificate,' the firelight turned his smile into something sardonic and wicked. 'You made things very easy for me.'

'Dion's why you married me, isn't he?' Joanna made it almost conversational, although she could feel a cold dew of perspiration on her forehead and her palms were wet. 'You wanted a son—any woman would have done provided she gave you that.' Her mouth closed firmly on the last word—the past was gone, so why stir everything up again? She could have told him exactly why he'd married her—it had taken a long time to sort out the tangled threads of the relationships between the other occupants of that Arcadian villa, but why tell him she had discovered all the ins and outs of it? Let it come as a surprise.

Better so; her head gave a little imperceptible nod. What she knew might come in useful, and it gave her a little thrill of excitement to realise that, like a fortunate gambler, she had an ace in her hand. She wasn't a silly, impressionable girl any longer, she had seen Arkady for what he was—a cold-hearted, scheming, calculating creature who would use anybody to get what he wanted. He'd fooled her at the beginning—but then she hadn't been so hard to fool—a girl in love never was!

'So,' he interrupted her thoughts, and her flicker of triumphant excitement dimmed a little, 'are you coming back with me, Joanna, or must I hire a nurse to care for the boy?' He was being quietly and cruelly implacable—he didn't care who he hurt as long as he had his son—and he thought he held all the cards. In one way, he was right—she tried to be fair. He could give Dion so much more of the good things in life than she could. Herself, she had never bothered much about money—she had never spent needlessly, so when the crunch came she had enough to see her through, and the small inheritance from her aunt in Bedford had meant she needn't worry about not working for a long time, at least until Dion started school—and she had the whip hand in another direction as well.

'Hire a nurse?' she sniffed. 'The sort of nurse

you'd need went out of fashion some time ago.' He raised his eyebrows and she finished triumphantly, 'A *wet*-nurse—they're hard to come by nowadays, and it's no use anybody waving a bottle at him because it's been tried. He won't have it!'

'Something of the sort could be arranged once we're home,' he pointed out. 'Some of the old ways still linger . . .'

'. . . Which would make for a very uncomfortable journey—besides, I won't allow it.' Joanna made it challenging, it was a bluff, but she hoped it would work. Arkady wasn't all that wealthy, but he could buy so much more than she could—instant flight to any part of the world, and she would never see Dion again. She would be left with nothing. She glanced at him and he held her gaze so that she knew she wouldn't win, and impotence bred an anger in her which brought her to an instant decision.

'Put like that,' she could feel herself going tight, heard Dion's little whimper as she gathered him too close, 'I don't seem to have all that much choice, do I? I don't doubt you could do exactly as you say—take him away from me, make it so I'd never see him again, but I won't allow that. Where he goes, I go, so you've no need to hire a nurse. Just tell me when you want us ready and we'll be waiting. Now you can go,' she added imperiously.

'And give you a chance to disappear again?' Arkady shook his head. 'Don't be a fool, Joanna— and that's what you *would* be if you think I'm one. We fly out to Athens tomorrow morning, so you'd better do what packing you need tonight.'

'You were that sure?' She let outrage spill over into her voice as she glared at him.

'Of course!' She could see his face, although the room was growing dim. The October sun had set and there was little light filtering through the drawn curtains. Arkady was smiling, a smile compounded of mockery and satisfaction.

'And you meant what you said,' she sounded disgusted. 'About taking him, the nurse and everything—you've arranged it all?'

'Down to the plane tickets,' he assured her smugly. 'You forget, I know you very well, we lived together for a year. —I can almost see that brain of yours going round in circles trying to find a way out, but there isn't going to be one. You both come back with me, since neither of you seems to be able to do without the other ... .'

'I've already agreed to that,' she reminded him promptly.

'. . . and I intend to see you carry it out, so give me the boy, I'll hold him for you while you push a few things in a bag and we'll be on our way.'

'We sit up in the airport all night?' she queried waspishly.

'Certainly not.' He had lit a fresh cigarette, but he ground it out on an ashtray in the hearth to hold out an imperative hand. 'Give,' he demanded, 'and do as I say. We'll spend the night at my hotel . . .'

'And you'll spend the night on guard outside my door, I suppose—or had you thoughts of shackling me to a radiator?'

'Neither.' Arkady gave her a swift grin—it lightened his face, made it less forbidding, but although Joanna had risen, she made no attempt to give him the child. Her eyes were wary. Arkady was a man it wasn't wise to trust too much—only as far as you could throw him. It didn't make her love for him any less, nothing could do that, but it made her suspicious.

'I'll get you a single room,' he offered, 'but the baby stays with me. That way, I'll know you'll both be there in the morning, because you wouldn't leave without him.'

'Don't be stupid,' she snorted. 'He'll want feeding again at seven o'clock, and if you think he'll last through the night on that, you've less sense than I thought you had. If I feed him again at midnight or thereabouts, he's still bound to wake up during the night, and *you* can't do anything for him!'

'Then we'll all have to stay together.' He raised an eyebrow mockingly, which effectually stilled the words on her tongue although her mouth remained open. 'Don't look so stunned, my dear. There are two single beds in my room and space to put a cot. I'll have the management install one. Now, go and get packed and then make a pot of tea.'

Reluctantly, Joanna handed the baby over to him, noticing that although he took the boy carefully, he handled him with confidence—but Arkady had always been confident at whatever he did—water-skiing, handling a boat, even building a wall—marriage too; he'd been confident about that, confident and competent. She hadn't equated confidence with experience at the time, that had come later, and with a sigh for her youthful stupidity, she went into the bedroom and banged about in the wardrobe and rattled through the drawers of the chest to fill a medium-sized suitcase.

That and a large box of disposable nappies was all she had to take with her, and the suitcase was more than half filled with Dion's bits and bobs—there wasn't much of her own in it. She had given away the maternity clothes, keeping only a couple of smock-shaped dresses, and she had been intending to buy herself a few new things, but with feeling so tired—and one couldn't take such a small baby shopping—she had put it off. Now she wished she hadn't. The smock dresses hung on her, making her look even thinner than she was, and even the cord trousers, the jeans and shirts she had saved from the previous year didn't fit properly.

Arkady handed over the baby as soon as her hands were free of the tea tray, and he frowned at her as she sat down while he poured.

'Is that the best you could do?' He indicated the dark green corduroy trousers and a plaid shirt with the tails not tucked in, and Joanna flushed. The straight-hanging shirt concealed the bunching where she had fastened a leather belt about her waist to keep her pants up.

'I'm thinner,' she said defensively, 'and I haven't had time to get anything new—it's difficult with Dion—the weather's not been good and I haven't got a pram yet . . .' She felt like crying, but it was only self-pity and the shock of seeing him again, so she choked down her tears and accepted the cup of tea he pushed into her hand. 'You said we were flying to Athens. Why Athens? I thought you'd have gone straight to Corfu.'

'I've got some business there, I was going to stay just one day, but I think we'd better make it a week. It'll give you a chance to have a rest and buy a few clothes, I'm not taking you home looking like that!'

CHAPTER TWO

JOANNA lay awake in the unfamiliar hotel bed, listening to the night noises—the occasional car speeding past. The hotel was somewhere behind the Albert Hall, she hadn't bothered to see where exactly, just noticed the dome of the building as the taxi had sped past. And there was the steady breathing of Arkady in the other bed and a snuffle now and then from Dion in his cot—she hoped he wasn't starting a cold.

One had to admire Arkady, even if only for his organising ability and sheer competence. The taxi he had ordered had been standing by, the meter ticking merrily away, but he hadn't appeared to hurry. Her landlady had been dealt with smoothly and competently, and when they had arrived at the hotel, so had the matter of a cot. Joanna recalled being anxious to please him when they had been together—apparently so did everybody else want to please him—it brought out his infrequent smile, a joy to behold.

Herself, she hadn't seen much of it, not after he had taken a good look at her in the brightly lit hotel foyer. He had hustled her swiftly to his room, carrying Dion himself nonchalantly as if it was an everyday thing. A lot of Englishmen wouldn't have been seen dead carrying a baby, but it didn't worry Arkady one bit. It was only when they were together in the privacy of the room that he had turned on her.

'What have you been doing to yourself?' he demanded. 'You're nothing but skin and bone, and your hair . . .!'

Joanna had shrugged and turned her back on him, disdaining a reply. Unhappiness, loss, misery—they wouldn't constitute a valid reason, not one he would be satisfied with, and in any case, she wasn't going to humble herself that far and there wasn't any physical reason she could quote.

He had put the sleeping baby down into the cot and turned her round so that the overhead light shone down on her pitilessly, emphasising her gauntness.

'You had a bad time, *agape mou*?' he nodded at the baby, 'with him?'

The little endearment caught at her heart, but she stood very still as his hand slid along her shoulder, feeling the sharpness of the bones through their thin covering of flesh.

'No worse than any other first-time mother,' she had answered baldly. 'Towards the end, it was rather wearisome—nothing to do but wait, and afterwards, one seems to take so long to get over it.' She would have liked to have said that loneliness had been the worst thing, but she wouldn't admit to a particle of weakness, not to him. 'I look terrible, I know, so I'd rather not go down to the dining room for dinner. Could I have it here? I can't leave Dion anyway.'

'We'll both have dinner up here,' and at her muffled protest, 'We stay together from now on, remember? You wouldn't leave me alone with him for a couple of hours, would you?' and at the swift shake of her head, 'and I won't leave you alone with him either. You've proved too slippery a customer in the past.'

Joanna had slumped wearily in a chair. 'Where could I go?'

'You'd think of something,' and there had been his smile to crimp her insides into knots as he had held her about the waist with one hand while he stripped the coverlet from one of the twin beds with the other. 'Lie down and rest while you can, the boy won't need you for another couple of hours—we might even be able to eat our dinner before he wakes.'

Later in the darkness, Joanna felt the sting of tears again. Why, oh, why did she have to keep rehashing what had been, and she tried not to hear the little voice in her mind that said, 'Because you don't want to think of the future. You'll think of anything but that!' Dion began his pre-'I want to be fed' grumbles and she looked at her watch, screwing up her eyes to decipher the illuminated dial. Two o'clock, but just right, he'd be due for a feed just before the plane took off.

Stealthily she slid out of bed, lifted Dion from his cot and slid back into bed again, feeling around in the darkness rather than switch on a lamp, but she needn't have bothered. Like a cat, Arkady slept with one eye open.

'Everything all right?' as he switched on his bedside lamp and looked across at her.

'Mmm.' She snuggled down with the baby. 'He's usually very good. Sometimes he sleeps right through till six, but he's been moved about a bit today, and it's upset him.' She watched as he slithered out of bed and crossed to the tea and coffee machine. 'Oh, for heaven's sake, put something on,' she muttered irritably, and turned her head away as Arkady came back to the bed and shouldered on the short robe that lay across the bottom of it. 'What are you doing, anyway?'

'Making you a drink. Elena always said that women should drink something at a time like this. Tea or coffee?'

'Knowledgeable,' she snapped.

'Well trained,' again that smile. 'I've been through it all before. One doesn't forget, not even after sixteen years! I've made you tea, coffee will keep you awake, and we've a busy day ahead.'

The flight was a charter one, not a regular service, and the rest of the plane was filled with what looked like an 'over fifties' holiday group taking an out-of-season package tour. Plump, motherly and grandmotherly women who had obviously spent the night with their new holiday hairdos protected by hairnets; well-cared-for husbands— one could almost smell the newness of shirts, socks and ties bought specially for this occasion— couples who didn't talk much because they knew each other so well they didn't need words. Joanna envied them their excitement and content.

She noticed Arkady eyeing them almost professionally and muttered as she drew off Dion's outer layer of clothing, a quilted one-piece suit that zipped up the front.

'Not suitable clients for your villas, I'm afraid, so you needn't look at them with a cash register expression.'

'Why?' Give Arkady his due, he sometimes paid attention to her opinion—he had only been in the holiday business for a couple of years whereas she had known it since she had left school. A photographer, yes, but when all the photos needed had been taken, she had worked at whatever she had been given, and often that had meant being a rep at a travel agency.

'They don't want peace and privacy, they want to see things,' she explained in a low murmur which only reached as far as his ear. 'They want a good hotel where they can all be together if they feel like it, shops where they can buy their souvenirs, sightseeing trips during the day with a decent courier and a bit of a dance when they get back in the evening, but a real dance to a real band—jigging about to disco music isn't their scene.'

'There are many of them?'

'Thousands! Darlings, aren't they? I remember being told that these were the backbone of the package tour industry. They save all year in order to see a bit of the world, and they really do see it. No sunbathing on beaches for them, they want to take snaps of "Dad at Pompeii" and "Mum by the Sphinx", things like that, and usually out of season. Lots of hotels rely on people like these to fill up in early spring or late autumn. Older people find the Mediterranean high summer far too exhausting. Has it given you an idea?'

'Mmm.' He was thinking about it, she could see that, and talking about business meant they couldn't talk about anything else. She needed to keep off the personal relationship thing—and it stopped her thinking about it.

Dion was being his usual lamblike self. Joanna had fed and changed him at the airport while they were waiting for the plane, and now, he was fast asleep—she wished she could sleep as well, but her mind was clamouring with questions. Perhaps a wise person would have left them unasked, waited to see rather than know beforehand, but—she gave a small sigh—she had never been wise, and surely it couldn't hurt to know if things were the same or if, by some miracle, they had changed. Diplomacy was the thing, so she started off on a comparatively safe topic.

'The villas, are they doing well?'

'Very well.' Arkady gave her a look that said he knew what she was up to but that he would play along if that was what she wanted, but he wouldn't make the game easy.

'How well?' Joanna knew the game, Arkady had played her at it a lot in the couple of months before she had run away—she would have to ask for every bit of information—she wondered why he got so much pleasure out of it.

'All of them booked solidly from the beginning of April right through to the end of October— more applications than there was time for.' He added a bit of extra information just as a makeweight. 'I have another six being constructed, they'll be ready for next spring.'

'On Corfu?'

'Kerkira,' he corrected, as he had corrected so many times before. 'It's the Greek name for the whole island, not just the town. Corfu is only used in the brochures because . . .'

'. . . because if you put "Kerkira" nobody would know where you meant,' she snapped.

'Give us time.' Arkady sounded long-suffering. 'We have to re-educate the world. You really want to know about the villas?'

'Yes,' she bit the word off between her teeth.

'Very well then, I'll tell you. Two on Paxos and the other four on Crete—we're extending, and if things go as well next year, we've bought some land on Rhodes, enough for a couple there.'

'*We?*' she queried.

'The registered company of St Vlastos and Son.' Arkady put out a long finger and touched Dion's cheek. 'He's very young to be a shareholder, but he'll grow.'

It wasn't any comfort to Joanna—to her, it meant Arkady had long-term plans for the baby, and she wondered what plans he had for her when Dion no longer needed her.

A stewardess came round with a trolley of in-flight drinks, but Joanna declined the gin and tonic Arkady ordered for her. 'Just the tonic, please,' she murmured as she passed the small bottle of gin across to him and poured the well chilled tonic water into her glass. 'It might upset him—the gin, I mean—quite a lot of things do.' But she had to find out more.

'Kore,' she queried softly, 'she must be nearly seventeen now. How is she?'

'In the throes of another grand passion.' Arkady told her sardonically. 'A water-skiing instructor, I believe. Ilone thinks a year at a finishing school in Switzerland will put a stop to these flights of high-flown romance. Strict supervision and the company of other girls of her own age—what do you think, would it be successful?'

Joanna pursed her lips primly, not because she was prim but more to stop herself saying exactly what she *did* think. Instead she tempered her thoughts. It was no business of hers, not any longer—she would try to be as cool and objective as her rising temper would allow.

'I never went to a school like that, but one thing I do know, and that is—girls can be strictly supervised for only part of the time, and while the mistresses may be strict, the girls generally take their lead from some other girl. You can vet the staff, but you can't vet the pupils, and usually the ringleader is one of the wild ones. Ilone,' there, she'd said the name and without a quiver in her voice, 'Ilone,' she repeated, just to be sure she could really say it at last, 'could be right, but on the other hand . . .' and she shrugged. 'Why don't you talk to Kore about it—ask her if it's what she'd like to do. She's old enough to start thinking for herself, you know,' she added sarcastically.

'She's old enough to be married,' there was a definite twinkle in his eyes, 'but it's been put off. She won't look at young Serghios, says he's got pimples and he's fat. His parents are beginning to wonder why the delay.'

'You Greeks!' Joanna exclaimed explosively, yet with a degree of resignation. 'When are you going to realise that the day of arranged marriages is over? You can't expect a spirited girl like Kore to meekly accept marriage with a young man she's only met a few times. Has he still got pimples?'

'Not so many,' now Arkady was smiling, 'and he's not so fat, but Kore doesn't know about it. She's refused to see him for the past six months. Every time his parents arrive, Kore goes missing— very embarrassing for them and for us.'

'Difficult,' Joanna said quietly as she shifted Dion from her right arm to her left—he was getting heavier every day and her arm was going to sleep. Inside, she didn't feel quiet, and perhaps, just perhaps, if they had been alone instead of in a plane full of people, she would have screamed at Arkady and told him, 'Send Ilone away instead of Kore!'

Ilone, the beautiful bitch who she had thought was some sort of relation—how stupid can you get? Joanna turned her head to the window, looking out and down as the panorama of the land so far below slid past. She didn't see anything, she couldn't; she was back in the past again, back to the day when her world had started to fall to pieces.

Arkady was going to Athens, some business matter, and at breakfast Ilone had begged a lift from him.

'Wonderful news!' she had waved a letter. 'Lisa, my friend in Athens, the one who has the boutique, she says some new clothes have come in from Paris and I so desperately need something new. You'll take me with you, Arkady?'

And that had been the first niggle. Arkady had said Joanna wouldn't want to go, a lonely day in Athens while he was at his business meetings—she wouldn't know what to do with herself—but he had right on his side, he was being practical. She didn't speak Greek, and she didn't know anybody, it would be a weary day. And she had gone to the top of the cliff to watch his sea-going cabin cruiser pull away from the marina and head south.

Afterwards, she had gone back to the villa and nodded understandingly when Anna the cook-general, had pantomimed a desire to go to Paleokastritsa to visit her son who ran a small restaurant there. She had watched Anna's black-clad figure stump off to catch the bus, amused that the old woman always seemed to know when the bus was coming, whereas she herself had never managed to catch a bus—perhaps they only ran for true-blue Corfiotes—and then she had looked for Kore, rather cross with Arkady for not offering to take his daughter with him.

But Kore had vanished—probably down to the marina, she would be back at lunchtime—only she wasn't, and by four in the afternoon, Joanna had started to worry in earnest. The only thing to do was to go and look for her—the few lessons she had made her confident, or nearly so, about driving the beach buggy.

She had found Kore at last, after a fruitless hunt through the holidaymakers on the beaches—in a beach cabin with a young Greek boy who worked on one of the day cruise boats. What happened after that hadn't been pleasant. Kore had been obstreperous, and the Greek boy had eased himself out of the door in an agony of embarrassment.

'Now see what you've done!' Kore had been wild with rage and everything had spilled out. How she and Stephanos were going to run away together. 'We'll come back, of course, and Papa will have to let us get married, and the Apostopolakis family can find another girl for their fat, pimply son!'

Joanna had tried reason, but it hadn't worked. Kore had faced her, red with rage and disappointment and with dark eyes full of spite.

'You—*you* try to tell me! You say I'm being stupid—it's you that's stupid! That's why Papa married you—because you're stupid! He doesn't love you, he loves Ilone—they've been lovers ever since she came here, after Mama died! Why else do you think they've gone to Athens together? She always goes with him, you wait and see if she doesn't!'

Joanna had tried some more, slightly gentler reason, but Kore had been too hysterical to more than listen.

'Papa doesn't love me, I'm a girl and I'm to be married off as soon as possible—and as for you, all he wants from you is a son. That's why he married you. He and Ilone will still be lovers.'

'Nonsense!' Joanna recalled being tart to cover he chill which had swept through her. 'Ilone's your aunt, and if your papa had wanted to marry her, he'd have done it years ago, after your mama died.' She had said it more to convince herself than Kore, but Arkady's daughter had an answer for that as well.

'She's not my aunt, only a sort of cousin of Mama's, and Papa would never marry her, she can't have any children!'

It had taken a lot of patience and even more soothing talk to get Kore back to the villa, fed and into bed, where she cried herself to sleep, and in the dark, empty place Joanna had sat shivering while she analysed the information. There *had* to be some small piece of truth in it—Kore couldn't have made it up out of the whole cloth.

She had spent a sleepless night, and even Kore's apology the next morning hadn't done much to help. The poison had festered inside her so that she read double meanings into the smallest thing and found herself becoming cold and unresponsive, irritable and suspicious. Everything was spoiled for her, and when Arkady, for the second time, went to Athens and Ilone went with him, this time to get her hair done properly—she said there wasn't a decent hairdresser on the whole of Kerkira—it had gone a long way to confirming Joanna's suspicions.

The final blow had come some time later. She had not been well, pregnant, although she hadn't realised it, and from the bedroom window she had seen Arkady and Ilone together in the moonlit garden—and this hadn't been hearsay or suspicion, she had seen with her own eyes Arkady put his arms round Ilone, seen Ilone's hands fluttering like white moths against the back of his head as he had kissed her, and watched as the two dim figures melted into one.

Proof positive, and the next day, she had acted, going in to Kerkira town on the bus, empty-handed except for her passport, her money and a few bits of underwear and clothes stuffed into a carrier bag. She had lied without hesitation—she had some things for the cleaners, she would have lunch, maybe go to the cinema, she wouldn't be too late back. But instead she had gone straight to the airport, taken the first available seat on a plane to London and sat like a statue all through the journey. Too miserable and lost to cry—that had come later.

And it had all been a waste of time and emotion, for here she was, going back to the same thing—Kore being difficult and Ilone still there. Arkady would probably try to get rid of his wife as soon as Dion was weaned, but this time he would find it difficult. She wasn't going to leave her son to Ilone. Let them be lovers, let them parade that love in front of her, she didn't care. She would not be parted from Dion, she and her son would either go or stay together! And she wouldn't be a fool any longer, not even though she still loved her husband. He would have nothing from her, she would share his house but not his bed. She would be a mother to Dion, but she wouldn't be a wife to her husband.

A lot of rustling of foil and the air hostess's bright, cheerful voice disturbed her, and Joanna blinked in surprise at how little time had passed. She had lived again through one of the most traumatic periods of her life and it had taken less than ten minutes! She didn't feel like eating the contents of the foil-wrapped package set in front of her, but she knew that to go without food would only make Dion irritable and windy, so she allowed Arkady to unwrap the foil and since she was hampered by only having one free hand and arm, he had to fork up the food for her.

The plane landed at Athens, and after passing through Immigration, Joanna watched the group of 'over fifties' hurrying away to their coach while Arkady hailed a taxi for the short drive into the city. She remembered how happy she had been the last time she had stayed in Athens and spoiled the memory by recalling it had all been play-acting on his part, but she didn't allow anything to show on her face, not even when the taxi drew up at the door of the same hotel they had stayed in before.

'Return to the scene of the crime,' she said tightly, and almost laughed aloud at the puzzled look on Arkady's face. Of course, he didn't know she knew—she would have to play this carefully, and she pinned a bright, meaningless smile on her face. 'They'll be able to serve me my dinner in my room?'

'A tray in bed, if you feel tired,' he even managed to sound sympathetic and caring. 'I shall have mine in the dining room.'

'You trust me that far?' She was surprised. 'I could take Dion and go while you were tucking in to your *souvlaki* . . . You were a lot more careful in London—or don't you think I dare?'

'Oh, I learn by experience.' He turned from fiddling about on the small table between the beds and waved the blue and gold-covered booklet at her. 'Your passport, *karthia mou*; you can't go anywhere without it. I'm taking it for safety's sake,' and Joanna watched impassively as he stowed it away in his wallet.

'Then I shall have to watch you, shan't I?' she snapped tartly. 'You can go anywhere, you could take Dion and leave me stranded here.'

The swift anger on his face shook her—she had never seen Arkady angry before—and his voice was harsh and chilly.

'You're letting an excess of mother love warp your judgment, *agape*. My son stays with me, and since you're his mother and he needs you, so do you. We stay together. You're my wife, and I don't much care whether you like it or not, it's something which I don't want altered. I'm not sure what made you run away before—could it have been boredom? But you won't have the chance to do it again . . .'

'I'm to be a prisoner?' she interrupted him fiercely.

'If you like to think of it that way,' he told her implacably. 'I suffered a good deal of humiliation at your hands—a man whose wife ran away from him. I won't be humiliated further, you understand?' He waited for a reply, but she refused even to look at him. This was a new side to Arkady, one she didn't know how to deal with yet, but she would learn!

'We made a mistake.' She lifted her chin. 'That's all! We should have been satisfied with a simple, uncomplicated holiday romance and left it at that.' If he still thought she didn't know about his affair with Ilone, she would leave him in ignorance. Rehashing it all would serve no good purpose; it would only increase the bitterness between them. 'We're from two different worlds,' she explained dully.

'And almost two different generations,' he added, but the anger had gone from his voice and he sounded rueful. Love made Joanna generous.

'You're not that much older than me—what is it, fourteen years? So stop talking as if you were my grandfather.' And to change the subject, 'I'm glad I brought my cameras, although I shall miss the little one you gave me. It was so easy to use, not like mine, and I've been taking photos of Dion—one a week while he's growing so fast.'

She was his wife and he had just said he didn't want that altered, so she would have to adjust. The thought of Arkady ever adjusting made her smile—he never could or would! And one couldn't live in gloom for ever, one had to make life bearable.

He caught the smile and crossed the room to her to take her hands in his, his fingers tracing the fine bones, twiddling her wedding ring which was very loose. 'We'll buy you a camera tomorrow, *agape*, before we buy you some clothes, so you can go on taking pictures. You brought the others with you, hmm?'

'Oh yes.' For a while there was peace between them. 'I'll show them to you while we have tea, if you like. They do serve tea here?'

That night and for every other night of their stay in Athens, they shared the same room, the twin beds divided by the impregnable barrier of Dion's cot. Joanna remembered what Arkady had said about humiliation, so she wouldn't humiliate him further by demanding a room to herself, and certainly not in a public place like an hotel. At the villa it would be different.

But there was a magic about Athens. She thought it came from the age-old stones of the Acropolis, and gradually she began to feel better, the tenseness drained away from her and she started to enjoy life once more. With a steady baby-sitter, one of the hotel maids, married and with children of her own so she knew what to do, Joanna went with Arkady on a small pilgrimage, retracing some of the ways they had trodden on their honeymoon.

She shook her head when he suggested a trip to Delphi, but as he pointed out, it was quite feasible. Dion wouldn't know about the journey by car, nor could he tell the difference between one hotel and another, so in the end they went, but not by road. Instead, Arkady took them by boat to Itea so that they could see, from the harbour, the two cliffs called the Shining Ones, and they spent the night in a painfully new tourist hotel where Dion, fast asleep and quite unaware, was crooned over by everybody on the staff. One thing Joanna learned—the Greeks loved children, and a porter who might carry up a suitcase with an ill grace almost begged for the task of carrying Dion.

There was a vast, incredible air of peace among the ruins of Delphi, as if all the prayers of all the pilgrims who had ever come to the shrine had laid a soft blanket around and among the fallen blocks of masonry, the broken pillars and all the ruins that occupied such a wide area. Joanna dropped on to the sunwarmed turf and felt the peace steal over her, washing away her hurt. She looked up at her husband, carrying the baby and quite unembarrased by it—so different from the men back home. If they could only stay here everything would work out and they would be happy again, but the ruins of Delphi were special, an oasis in a mad world, and nobody could stay here forever.

Tomorrow they would leave for Corfu and all the hurt would come streaming back, and there, in the villa at the top of the cliffs, she would be back in the whirlpool again. Arkady's mistress would give her a false kiss of welcome, pretend she was glad to see her return, and there would be Kore with her young eyes full of a knowledge she was too youthful to cope with.

CHAPTER THREE

ARKADY brought them to Kerkira town—Joanna still insisted on calling it Corfu; that way, it meant something to her—in an air taxi from Athens. She had raised her eyebrows at the cost, but he shrugged it aside.

'It's a long journey by sea, long and tedious, on one of the ferries, and it would also mean an extra journey first, to Patras. Besides, it's getting late in the year, and we could run into a storm. This way is both quicker and better.'

'You explain things so beautifully,' she said waspishly, and then regretted it as her eyes fell on the set of new suitcases and she thought of what they contained—a nearly complete wardrobe of clothing suitable for the winter on Corfu, including some gorgeous Italian separates and the beautiful trousers which had the advantage of covering and hiding the appalling thinness of her legs—and Arkady had borne with her spats of temper very well, she reminded herself. In fact, if it wasn't for her periodic bouts of nastiness, they would have got along very well.

But she considered that she was entitled to be nasty if she felt like it—she was the injured party. Betrayed by a practised adulterer—forced to flee, to set up home alone and be alone when she had her baby, and then dragged back willy-nilly. But the practised adulterer didn't seem to see things her way, he tended to act as though *he* was the injured party! That she was the one to be forgiven, but only when she had salved his pride and she had learned her lesson!

The little airport was quiet and nearly empty when they passed through, and Arkady's transport, a white Range Rover, was waiting for them in the car park. A bit dusty but otherwise unharmed. That was one of the good things about Corfu—a vehicle could be left anywhere, it wouldn't be vandalised. And not just in Corfu. Joanna recalled a trip they had taken, soon after they had been married. Arkady had driven this same vehicle into Piraeus and finding the car parks full, had left it in a side street. They had been away for several days, visiting the Cyclades, and yet, when they had returned, the Range Rover had been still in the same place and quite untouched, not a mark on its immaculate paint work.

'An hour and we'll be home.' He strapped her in carefully, apparently unaware that, to her, his would-be comforting remark was more in the nature of a threat. The thought of being welcomed by Ilone, receiving a Judas kiss on her cheek, was almost more than Joanna could stand—but she would have to stand it—and Kore, how would Kore take it?

They headed north, passed through Gouvia and then turned west for Paleokastritsa. There were still quite a lot of late holidaymakers about, but the roads no longer buzzed with mopeds and scooters and they had the winding mountain road to Markrades to themselves, which was just as well. The hairpin bends had always scared Joanna to death, and her arms tightened round Dion and she bent over him protectively as if she would shield him from harm.

At Krini, the narrow, poorly surfaced road gave
out and they continued along what was no more
than a track worn through the vegetation that
clothed the clifftops. Joanna caught sight of the
ruins of the Byzantine fortress of Angelocastro in
the middle distance and wondered how she could
have forgotten how close to the villa it was.

And they weren't expected. Nobody came
running as the Range Rover drew up beside the
villa, burying its bonnet in a large bush of
rosemary—because that was where the rosemary
had always been and nobody had ever thought to
move it.

'I'll carry him myself.' Joanna was like a she-
wolf with a lone cub as Arkady helped her down
from the high vehicle and she looked through the
arcading on to the deserted patio with a jaundiced
eye. 'No welcoming committee; I'm disappointed!'

'No chance.' His stern face relaxed into a rueful
smile. 'The telephone wasn't working. I tried
several times until the operator told me the lines
were out of order.'

'When are they *not* out of order?' Joanna was
determined nothing should give her any pleasure.
She wouldn't soften, not one bit. It was best to
start as one meant to go on. There was an
abandoned lounger on the patio, and she gave a
brisk 'tut-tut' as they passed it—the cushions at
one end were stained with rain, and then there was
a light patter of feet, the door was flung open and
Kore stood there; little changed by the year that
had passed since Joanna had seen her last. Maybe
she had grown a couple of inches, but that was all.
Words spilled out of her as if she had been holding
them back too long.

'Papa! You're back, and with Joanna and the baby!' She drooped an eyelid. 'I've kept the secret, truly I have, but I'm sure Ilone knows. If she does, it wasn't me who told her!' Her young face was alive with curiosity as she detached herself from her father and advanced on her stepmother. 'Welcome home, Joanna, and my brother Dion,' her urgent fingers parted the shawl and she peeped down at the small head with its covering of black fluff. 'Oh, isn't he tiny! Can I hold him?'

Joanna had been afraid Kore would be jealous. It had seemed more than a possibility. The girl had always been so scathing about just being a girl and therefore of little importance except to be married off, but Kore was no actress and her face mirrored her feelings. She looked glad, she *was* glad.

'And Anna said the cot would be too big for him,' she went on, 'the crib would be better.' Arkady had gone back to the car to bring in the suitcases and Kore touched Joanna's arm. 'I *am* glad you're home again, Jo—I've missed you. Papa's been away such a lot and it's been very dull here.'

Joanna's lips twitched. 'I thought I heard your papa saying something about a water-skiing instructor who was occupying a lot of your time?' She handed Dion over and flexed her arm which had gone dead with carrying him all this time.

'I have to pass the time somehow, don't I?' Kore lifted her chin and said it in a pathetic attempt at grown up sophistication. 'Oh, I'll tell you about it later, Ilone's coming down the stairs now,' and carrying the baby carefully, she called up to the small, slender woman who had halted on the third step from the bottom, to give a swift glance

around the hallway before she turned a tight smile
on Joanna, who went on rubbing her arm while
she absorbed the shock of the inimical gaze from a
pair of doelike dark eyes which were as hard as
stone.

'The wanderer has returned.' Joanna knew it
was the wrong thing to say and her light, jesting
tone was equally wrong, but she couldn't help it.
'Bearing, or rather Kore's bearing, the fruits of my
endeavours.' Arkady must be garaging the car, he
was taking one hell of a time bringing in the
suitcases, and without him standing by, she felt
rather like a lamb left tethered in the presence of
a wolf.

Of course, Ilone looked nothing like a wolf. A
small, slender woman, dark-haired, dark-eyed,
with a face like a madonna and the figure of a
wood nymph, she didn't look anything like thirty-
three or four. In a poor light, she looked little
older than Kore. Joanna appreciated the stance on
the third step, it made Ilone look like a marble
goddess mounted on a plinth. This way, she could
look down on Joanna. The madonna face smiled,
red lips parted to show small, even white teeth,
and Ilone spoke.

'I'd given up ever expecting to see you again,
Joanna, but we welcome you.'

'I bet you do!' Joanna gritted her teeth silently.
Was she supposed to go down on her knees, abase
herself, beg pardon for her sins? Her thoughts ran
on. It was a pity Ilone ever had to resort to speech,
her voice wasn't as pleasing as the rest of her.
Even when, as now, she spoke softly, it had a hard
grating quality that jarred.

'Thanks,' she muttered, the word dropping

grudgingly into the silence, but she needn't have
bothered. Arkady was coming through the door
with the suitcases—she could tell by the way
Ilone's gaze concentrated on a spot behind her.
Joanna was about to be ignored.

'My dear!' Ilone descended the three steps—she
didn't mind if Arkady looked down on her.
'You've been gone so long. We thought you were
never coming back,' and her small, ringless hands
fluttered out to him as she passed Joanna without
a glance and went to greet him.

Dismissed! Joanna allowed herself a smile. Just
as though she was an errant housemaid, rebuked
for some fault and then passed by as the lady went
on to greet another, more worthy person.

Aside, she caught up with Kore. 'Shall we take
Dion upstairs? He's been carried a lot today and I
expect he'll need changing.'

'Oh yes, let's!' Her stepdaughter was full of
enthusiasm. Joanna wondered how long it would
last. 'We can see if the crib's big enough—I hope
so, because Anna's had me making new muslin
ruffles for it. It hasn't been used for so long, the
old ones were quite yellow. Just fancy! This is my
brother. D'you know, Jo, I always thought I'd
hate a brother on sight, but I don't. He's so tiny
and helpless and I don't envy him a bit. See,' as
they entered the big bedroom, 'we've put the crib
by the side of the bed so you can get at him easily
if he wakes during the night—and isn't it clever of
me, remembering which side of the bed you slept
on?'

'Very clever,' Joanna said absentmindedly as she
crossed to the far door which opened on to a small
dressing-room and peeped inside. The narrow bed

was still there, and Kore heard her soft grunt of satisfaction.

'Oh, Jo! You're not going to put him in there, are you? He'll be all by himself and you mightn't hear him if he cries.'

'Not Dion, your father.' Joanna bit her tongue to stop the words coming out. Somebody was going to sleep in here, either Arkady or herself, she didn't care which. But it would be a purely private thing—she felt generous enough to spare Arkady any further humiliation, even considering how he had humiliated her!

'Dion cries sometimes,' she explained smoothly. 'I just wanted to see if there was anywhere I could take him. I wouldn't want him to keep your papa awake all night, and he's quite capable of doing just that. Now, tell me what you've been doing while I've been away.'

'Papa said I could work, if I could find a job.' Kore plumped down on the bed, next to Joanna, and watched as she undressed the baby. Out of the corner of her eye Joanna noticed a small, triumphant smile touch her stepdaughter's mouth and press a dimple in her cheek. 'So I found myself one, down at the marina in Paleokastritsa—mostly taking bookings for water-skiers and boat trips, but it wasn't much fun, so I went to one of the hotels as a receptionist. That was better. When we were busy, I had to do all sorts of things—make beds, wait on tables—I think that was the best job, being a waitress. People gave me lovely big tips!'

'And of course you needed the money.' Joanna's mouth twitched into laughter. 'How old are you now, Kore?'

'Sixteen and a bit.' The girl straightened Dion's

wrappings and touched his cheek with a gentle finger. 'The age, Papa says, when people should start to accept a bit of responsibility. Anna's making tea, I heard Papa ask her to. Would you like me to bring yours up here?'

'No, thank you, dear.' Joanna came to an immediate decision. She was not here of her own free will and maybe she wasn't much welcome, but she was damned if she was going to skulk in a bedroom. 'I'll put Dion in his crib, wash my hands and face and come downstairs.'

'*Endaxi.*' Kore sprang to her feet and headed for the door. 'I'll help Anna—all part of the "responsible person act", you know.' Her young face wore a droll look as she let herself out on to the wide balcony that ran the whole length of the upper floor.

Left to herself, Joanna settled Dion in the crib. He didn't need feeding for at least an hour—and she looked down at his sleeping face with an emotion which was almost idolatrous. He looked so beautiful, and he was such a good baby. She went into the bathroom to clean herself up. She gazed wistfully at the bath, almost put the plug in and turned on the taps—but water was precious on Corfu, every drop used in the house had to be brought by tanker and pumped into the enormous cistern that lay beneath the patio. In any case—she went to the bathroom door and peeped into the bedroom—Arkady hadn't brought the cases up yet. Probably too busy greeting Ilone—so she couldn't change. She'd have a quick shower before dinner and change then.

Meanwhile, she'd wash off the travel stains and hope that cherry red linen trousers, a silk shirt of a paler shade of the same red and soft, comfortable sandals would do.

When she returned to the bedroom, Arkady was there, stooping over the crib, and she hurried forward to plant herself between him and the baby, as if the child was in need of defence.

'He's all right,' she said truculently. 'He should sleep for another hour at least, I don't want him disturbed.'

'Just looking.' He straightened up and smiled down at her, a smile so small it was hardly noticeable. 'Is everything all right for you? The crib, is it on the correct side, the side you'll be sleeping?'

Joanna turned away, went to the dressing table and started to flick a powder puff over her face. In the mirror, her eyes met his. 'I shall be sleeping in the middle of the bed,' she said airily. 'So it doesn't matter which side the crib's on, does it? Or if you prefer,' she jerked her head in the direction of the dressing-room, 'I can shift the crib in there and use the single bed for myself.'

She watched idly as his face hardened into an expressionless mask, it meant he was losing his temper and trying to conceal it, but she felt very brave. 'Start as you mean to go on, is my motto,' she added, 'and that's what I'm doing!'

'So I have a wife who refuses to be a wife . . .'

'Got it in one!' This was easy, and triumph welled up in her. 'But don't be afraid it might be the subject of gossip—nobody will know about it except ourselves. You needn't worry about any more public humiliation. Outside of this room, I shall play my part—while Dion and I are here. I shall be the perfect wife, but behind this door, you could say we'll be poles apart.' It was going so well, it seemed a shame to stop there. 'You mentioned your humiliation when we were in Athens—how you suffered as a Greek male whose wife had walked out on him. Well, let me tell you, *your* humiliation was nothing to mine! Why else did you think I'd walked out?'

Arkady could move like lightning when he wanted to, and apparently this was one of the times when he wanted to. A couple of strides brought him to stand behind her and he grasped at her shoulders, turning her round forcibly to face him.

'Your humiliation!' His normally quiet voice grated on her ears. 'What was that? An idiocy you dreamed up? I know pregnant women have these fancies . . .'

'I didn't dream anything up,' Joanna snorted in disgust, 'and as for fancies, I didn't know I was pregnant, so how could I have them?' Then she shut her mouth firmly, wrinkling her nose as though there was a bad smell somewhere.

'And what was I supposed to have done?' He wasn't shouting, he didn't have to—his face was so close to hers she could feel his warm breath on her cheek.

'As if you need telling!' Joanna wanted to shrink away from the blaze in his dark eyes, but pride held her rigid. 'Oh, I know,' she went on while she still had the courage, 'it probably didn't mean much to you—it wouldn't be important to a man, they do it all the time . . .'

'I see.' His hands tightened on her shoulders and she winced at the pain his fingers were causing. 'I've been unfaithful, is that it?'

'Speaking for myself,' she said haughtily, 'and for the last year, I wouldn't know and I don't care—but before that, *yes*! And don't bother to deny it, because I wouldn't believe you.'

'And how did you come by this knowledge?' He raised his eyebrows mockingly. 'A little bird whispered in your ear, perhaps?'

Some remaining spark of wisdom shone through her temper. It would never do to involve Kore—she'd have to give it all, chapter and verse. Arkady would get it all out of her and his daughter would suffer—besides, Kore had shown signs of being friendly, and heaven only knew, Joanna needed any friend she could get during the coming months. Knowing her husband and his devotion to his business, she would be very much on her own. She could look forward to a long, cool and very wet period when she would be confined to the house.

Coping with Ilone's barely concealed hostility would be enough, she didn't want Kore to think she had let her tongue wag too freely. The pressure of Arkady's fingers increased and he shook her.

'Tell me!'

'Nobody told me.' She tried to wriggle away from the grasp of his hands. 'Nobody needed to. I've got eyes and I used them. Oh yes, I admit they weren't open much when you first brought me here, I was a romantic fool living in a haze, but that stopped very soon and I began to question. My infatuation with you had a very short life.'

He let her go quite suddenly, and with relief she turned back to the mirror, but even there she wasn't free of him. His face was reflected alongside hers, dark, hard and severe.

'And your questions were answered with what?'

'Reason.' To keep her hands occupied, she picked up the hairbrush and began pulling it through her hair while she tried for a bit of sophistication. 'Things didn't gel, if you know what I mean.'

'I had an American mother, I'm quite familiar with slang,' Arkady pointed out. 'Yes, I know what you mean—what things?'

'When I knew the set-up,' drawled Joanna as though she was full of confidence, while inwardly she was quaking. 'The way you Greeks do things,' she waved the hairbrush airily, 'that was when I started thinking things out. Why should you have married me? That was what I asked myself. I had no dowry, no influential family, I couldn't be of any help to you in getting your business off the ground . . .'

'I thought I told you I loved you.'

'Pooh!' she retorted scornfully. 'Whenever did a Greek allow a little thing like love to influence him when it's a matter of business? Why should I think it would influence you in my favour when I see the way you try to manipulate your own daughter— trying to marry her off to a young man she neither likes nor cares about for purely business reasons? As for me, I suppose you thought I was a romantic fool with so many stars in my eyes I wouldn't see where I was going—that and the fact I'd probably be reasonably good breeding stock, of course.'

'You've no reason . . .'

'Yes, I have!' she broke in almost hysterically. 'I saw you, remember. I *saw* you!'

'You saw me? When? Where?'

'And wouldn't you like to know?' It was the

nearest she could get to a sneer. 'I'm not telling, it's something you can ponder in the still watches of the night—*alone* in your bed!'

'You damned little spitfire!' There was something like admiration in his eyes, but it vanished before she could be sure, to be replaced by a hard gleam as he jerked her closer to him—so close she could feel the warmth of his body through the thin stuff of her shirt.

'But I shan't be alone,' he was murmuring as he fended off a threatened blow from the hairbrush and dodged the second by moving his head away just in time. 'You are my wife, Joanna, and while you're here in my house, you'll sleep in my bed. You call me a Greek husband, then I'll be one—the master in my own home.'

'You'll force me?' She licked lips which had gone dry with fear. 'I'll scream the house down,' she threatened.

'And nobody will interfere,' he told her emphatically. 'Nobody would dare, not between a man and his wife. For however long you stay here, you'll be my wife in every sense of the word—and if you don't like the prospect, I'll drive you into Kerkira, buy you a ticket and put you on the first plane back to England. The child will stay here and we'll manage with him somehow. Ilone will find a woman who'll nurse him, or I'll get . . .'

Joanna didn't wait to find out what he'd get. The very mention of Ilone's name made her shake with rage. 'No, you won't!' she spat. 'He's *my* baby! Very well,' her defiance collapsed, 'I'll stay and we'll play it your way, and a lot of joy you'll get out of it!'

'Oh, we both will.' He pulled her even closer

and, like a rabbit hypnotised by a stoat, she watched as his face came down to meet hers. 'Close your eyes if you can't stand the sight of me,' she heard him mutter through the thunder of the blood in her ears, and then his mouth was on hers, hard, cruel, forcing her lips apart, and she steeled herself not to respond. It wasn't a caress, it was a punishment—he was hurting her, bruising her mouth, and he knew it; it seemed to give him a kind of unsatisfactory satisfaction.

Drearily, Joanna found herself wondering how long she could hold out. There was a faint taste of blood on her tongue and her lower lip was smarting—she supposed it had split under the barbaric pressure, but some part of her was almost triumphant. Arkady still wanted her—just wanting, not loving, or—behind her closed eyelids she felt the prick of tears—maybe he'd been on some self-denial stint.

The bruising pressure eased against her mouth, although his hands still held her firmly, and against her will she could feel herself responding to the sensuous thrust of his hips against her. He raised his head, shook her a little until she opened her eyes to see his, slitted and dark with knowledge, gleaming down at her.

'It's been a long time, *karthia mou*,' he murmured, 'and it's still there, isn't it!' He was only holding her with one arm now and his free hand was picking at the buttons that fastened her shirt. 'Shall we miss going down for tea?'

Hot colour rushed to her cheeks as his fingers caressed her breasts, only to drain away swiftly, leaving them paper-white. Her voice, when she could trust herself to speak, surprised her. It was quite cool, although there was a faint breathiness at the back of it as though she'd been running fast and hard.

'No,' she didn't put any emphasis on it, just made it dull and matter of fact. 'I'm thirsty and Dion will need feeding soon, so I'd like something to drink before he wakes,' and with steady fingers she brushed away his intrusive hand to do up the buttons Arkady had undone before she turned away to look at herself in the mirror. She smoothed her hair and frowned at her swollen lower lip while she unscrewed the cap of her lipstick with remarkably steady hands.

'But you want me, my dear.' He was smiling and she thought she detected triumph in the gleam of his eyes and the curl of his mouth. She longed to wipe that smile from his face!

'So?' she shrugged, assuming a sophistication that turned the word into a bitter irony. 'Want will have to be my master, won't it?' Suddenly she was no longer passive, needing to let him know what it was like to be a woman alone. 'What did you expect?' she demanded quietly but with venom. 'I've lived like a nun for a year. It's quite reasonable I should want, but I don't have to give way to purely animal instincts—I'm a thinking and reasoning human being, not a bitch in season.' She swung round to face him, surprised it was so easy to be blunt, even a little crude. 'I've often wanted in the past year, but I've found an infallible cure for it. I make a cup of tea, take an aspirin and have a quiet think about men, especially the ones who so gaily break their marriage vows. After about five minutes of that, the wanting goes away and I can only feel disgust. Now, shall we go down

before the damn stuff's too cold to drink? We're
late enough as it is!'

Joanna knew she had spent far too long with
Dion, but after he had been fed and done up in his
sleeping suit, she had played with him. He was
truly smiling now, he even managed a wide
chuckle of pleasure when she tickled his tummy, so
she was late and her suitcases hadn't been
unpacked. Underwear was easy, it was in the
smallest of the cases, so she helped herself to a
handful and went to take a shower—a very quick
one, because she'd forgotten to ask whether the
cistern was running low.

Arkady walked into the bedroom to find her
pulling on the trousers of an ensemble which had a
definitely Oriental air about it—plain dark green
satin trousers covered by a hip-length cheongsam-
shaped top in a paler green and embroidered
lavishly with pink and gold butterflies. 'Very
becoming,' was his comment, 'and your hair's
beginning to look a little better. Shall I brush it for
you?'

'No, thanks.' She gave an inward shiver of
pleasurable dread. Love, real love, didn't die—you
could ignore it, shut it away behind a locked door,
but when you opened the door, it was still there,
alive and ready to claw at you—and her love for
Arkady was the real thing in her life and it
wouldn't go away and be dead. Worst of all, she
suspected he knew this, and she could dissemble
till she was black in the face and he'd see through
her futile stratagems.

'Please, leave me alone,' she muttered, but the
hairbrush was already in his hand and he was

pushing at her gently to sit down. 'We're late enough already,' but there wasn't much force in her protest, 'and you know how——' she had been going to say 'Ilone' but changed it swiftly '—how Anna hates it when the food is ready and we're not . . .' Her voice died away as Arkady arranged a towel about her shoulders and began brushing, long, even strokes which had an hypnotic effect on her, and misery welled up into a tight knot in her throat. This was how it had used to be—was it only a year ago? It seemed more like a lifetime—a long, cold, drab period when she had ached for the touch of his hand and the warm strength of his body against hers.

'I had a shower,' she heard herself babbling hysterically. 'I hope it was all right. I meant to ask if we were low on water, but each time, I forgot . . .' A little snuffle from the crib brought her back rudely to the present. Arkady could charm the birds from the trees when he wished— Joanna had been charmed once and she had learned her lesson. With a gasp, she pushed his hands away and sped across to her son, Arkady following, and they both stood looking down at the child.

Dion was fast asleep, but his eyebrows twitched so that, for a second, he looked heartbreakingly like his father. 'Nothing wrong there,' came his father's voice.

'And what do you know about it?' Joanna pushed him aside to get nearer to the crib. 'He's got wind. I'm not coming down to dinner, you can send somebody up with a tray for me, I'm staying with him.'

'Stupid!' He glanced down at her bare feet and

then at the pair of cork-soled green satin slippers standing ready by the bed. 'Get your shoes on and we'll go. Oh yes!' as her mouth opened to defy him. 'I've had more practice with babies than you—remember? Although she's growing up, Kore was a baby once. The boy will be all right, a little bit of wind isn't going to kill him.'

'Ha!' She remained stooping over the crib. 'So much experience, how you men like to kid yourselves! You proposed to take him away from me before he was weaned. Dion can do without your type of experience, thank you . . .'

'But you can't do without your dinner,' he broke in on her angry tirade. 'And you can't spend the next few months up here in the bedroom with him. Now let me see—Anna has a granddaughter, Sylvie; she's only about twelve, but she has got experience. I believe she has at least five brothers and sisters, all younger than herself. We'll send for her tomorrow, and if she's suitable she can look after the boy for you.'

'Not until I've seen her, so don't make plans without consulting me,' she snapped. 'I know it's one of your things, this desire to run everybody's lives for them, but you're not running mine—or Dion's. A twelve-year-old child!' she snorted. 'She should be in school!'

'Sylvie can read and write and she can use the adding machine in the local shop. She's often at the till, and there aren't any complaints—she has finished with school and she will come during the day so that you may have some time to yourself.' Arkady tapped her hand. 'Joanna, are you listening to me?'

'Not much!'

'Then listen harder. The child's father is an invalid, the family need the money and they're Greek, too proud to accept charity.'

'Very well,' Dion hadn't woken and she turned away, 'I'll have a look at her, if that's what you want, but I won't . . .'

'Of course not,' he put an arm about her and pulled her towards the door, 'but I think you'll find her quite satisfactory. She speaks a little English.'

The hinged, louvred shutters that separated the dining-room-cum-lounge from the patio were folded back, as were the solid, outside shutters, and only the screen doors and the heavy curtains kept out the damp breeze. Joanna remembered those curtains, they were one of the few things about which she had had her own way when she had lived here before. It had been a bit of a fight to get them, nothing physical or violent—Ilone didn't go in for that—only passive resistance, which was much harder to combat. Joanna calculated she had wasted more than a month in reasoned argument before she had ordered the damn things and had them hung and another month of having to draw them in the evenings before Ilone stopped complaining gently about the amount of dust they would hold and how much extra work they gave old Anna.

There was a log fire on the stone hearth, and this, together with the light from the candles on the branched candelabrum on the dining table, was all the light provided. Joanna peered into the gloom as she came through the door, blinked and reached a hand to the switch that controlled the ceiling lights. She snapped it down and the room sprang to life under the brilliant illumination. Company for dinner, and she examined the stranger swiftly. Young, male—too young for Ilone but too old for Kore; but her stepdaughter's eyes were regarding him with an expression of fatuous devotion.

CHAPTER FOUR

ILONE was wearing white silk jersey draped like an ancient Greek chiton, even to the cross-bandings that emphasised her full breasts, and her feet were shod in modern, comfortable copies of the ancient sandals that matched the gown. Joanna returned the rather bleak smile with which she was greeted and thought that Ilone resembled nothing so much as a Wedgwood figurine lifted off its plate—the spirit of spring, or something like that.

And yes, Kore had certainly earned some money—the dress she was wearing looked like a model. A simple white linen shift which barely covered her knees—so simple, it had to have been expensive, and embroidered all over with small spires of delphiniums in different shades of blue. Not the sort of dress Ilone would have bought for her, Ilone tended to the young look for Kore—with frills! Beneath the hem of the dress, Kore's long, slender legs—she was going to be tall, like her father—shimmered in sheer silk, and she had emphasised their length with very high-heeled sandals.

Joanna walked forward, conscious of her husband beside her and with a hand lightly resting at her waist. She felt a faint squeeze of his fingers and put on a wide smile, while her stepdaughter went through the introductions with a great deal of aplomb.

'A friend, Papa, Hank Sommers. We met at the

hotel where I worked. Hank, this is my papa and my stepmama.'

It was a surprise, and it could have been worse, that was Joanna's first thought as she shook hands formally and felt a gigantic Alma Mater ring cut into her fingers. Hank could have been a hippy, but he was no such thing—he was the typical all-American boy, from the top of his blond crew-cut to the thick rubber soles of his loafers, with a wide open, almost ingenuous face and a soft drawl that shrieked of Mammy and the old plantation; moreover—she winced as she rubbed her fingers surreptitiously—he was the muscular type. His well worn but scruplously clean shirt—not a tee-shirt—fitted his shoulders as if it had been shrunk to them.

In that case, Joanna couldn't understand the little prickle of dismay that slid down her back like an ice cube. Of course, he wasn't a boy, up close he looked older—perhaps that was the reason. She flicked a glance at her husband, who was having his hand—literally—wrung, but Arkady was, as usual, giving nothing away. His face was bland and she couldn't read what was going on behind his dark, inscrutable eyes, but at least he wasn't in a temper at being saddled with an unexpected guest on his first night home. But then Arkady was a Greek, and to him, a stranger and a guest were the same thing; the same word was used for both.

Ilone preserved a dignified silence—no doubt worrying about the effect this would have on the Apostolakis family; word was bound to reach them. They might even decide that Kore wasn't a suitable wife for their Serghios—which would be in the nature of another humiliation for the St

Vlastos family. Betrothed young girls did not invite other boy-friends to dinner—they didn't *have* other boy-friends!

Joanna shrugged off this little worry over dinner. She had enough of her own troubles to worry about, and when, after dinner was over, Kore produced a photograph album, she was lured to sit between her stepdaughter and Hank as Kore displayed photographs, pointing out the ones Joanna had taken.

'Gee, they're good!' Hank exclaimed enthusiastically, 'but then you're a professional, aren't you, ma'am? I do a bit myself, but strictly amateur, I've got a Rolliecon—what do you use?'

Joanna heard herself explaining about her Hasselblad which she used for inside work, the Nikon which was better for exterior shots and the little Canon for snaps, while she cast one anxious eye at Arkady and Ilone and kept the other one on her watch. Greek dinners went on for ever, they had stayed much longer at table than she had expected, and she finally decided she dared stop no longer and with a murmured excuse and another bruising handshake from Hank, she fled upstairs to give Dion his supper.

Halfway through the feed, she heard the sound of a car leaving the grounds, and then Arkady was coming through the door and standing over her.

'I don't know whether to give that child a smacked bottom or pin a medal on her,' he said with a fleeting smile.

'She's very like you,' Joanna muttered ungraciously. 'Obstinate and intent on getting her own way. She's trying to show you she isn't a child any longer.'

'And you approve of her taste in young men?'

'Taste is a matter of choice, and she hasn't got much choice, has she? That was the water-skiing instructor, I suppose?'

'Mmm.' Arkady was busy putting the contents of his pockets, cigar case, lighter and loose change, on the bedside table, 'And you haven't answered the question.'

'What purpose was there in asking it?' she fired up. Dion was asleep in her arms, and she was deathly tired—she felt she couldn't see straight any longer. All she wanted to do was to take her baby and crawl into some dark, private hole where nobody could get at her—she had enough troubles of her own without getting involved in teenage infatuations. 'Why ask me?' she demanded irritably. 'I'm no expert when it comes to judging men—Look at the mess I've made of *my* life!'

'You're tired.' He bent over her to take the baby and when her arms tightened, 'No, don't let's fight over him, he's my son as well as yours and I'm quite capable of putting him in his crib. Have a shower and put yourself to bed.'

Joanna looked at the wide expanse of handworked crochet which comprised the bedspread and at the lace-trimmed pillows before her gaze slid to the back of her husband's dark, well-shaped head, and her mouth went dry while her tongue seemed to swell to double its size, making speech of any sort impossible. In any case, even if she had managed to find the right words and get them out so that they could be understood; pride made it impossible for her to beg, and his threat to send her back to England while keeping the baby here on Corfu was still fresh in her mind.

Arkady wouldn't have made the threat if he hadn't meant it—a little thing like a woman's tears would have no effect on him. He had said he would do it—he *would* do it. And to think that less than a couple of years ago she had admired his unwavering determination!

With a gulp of despair, she caught up her night things and her shower cap and made her way to the bathroom. She no longer cared whether there was enough water or not—she rather hoped she would use it all, to the very last drop, as she hung nightdress and robe on a hook and stepped out of her clothes to leave them untidily in a heap on the floor. She turned the shower on full so that the spray battered at the plastic of her cap as she stood beneath it. Her very own private Armageddon was approaching, and although she wasn't ready for it, she could at least be clean!

The rings of the curtain rattled as he parted them and stepped into the shower beside her. She dropped the cake of soap and tried to hide herself behind an inadequate bath sponge.

'Don't look so appalled, *koritse*.' His voice, though low, was perfectly audible over the noise of the water and the thunder of her heartbeat. 'We've done this before and I've given you plenty of time, more than a week to get used to the idea . . .'

'I'll never be used to it,' she gasped against his chest as he pulled her into the circle of his arm and with his free hand slopped bath gel over her shoulders and began smoothing it down her back. 'Never, *never*!'

Seriously, he went on soaping her, and she could feel her skin scorching where he touched it. 'If you felt like that, you should have accepted my other offer—your flight back to England.'

'You knew I wouldn't.' The touch of his hands was an agony and she thought she might die of it. 'I wouldn't, I couldn't—my baby . . .' It was all getting muddled in her mind, she was trembling uncontrollably with a mixture of hate and love, and both seemed to have the same effect on her, making her weak and despondent.

'You love me, Joanna.' There was no sweet endearment to soften it this time, it was just a bald statement. 'You're a good mother, you love your child and you love me.'

Joanna was long past being able to explain the mixed-up emotions she was feeling—the delight and dread of having him close to her, that she was fascinated and repelled at the same time by her reaction to the touch of his thigh against her own, the sound of his heartbeat beneath her cheek.

He tipped her face up to his and she felt the touch of his lips on her forehead, felt the blaze of them as they trailed down her cheek to find her mouth, forcing her own lips apart and invading but so gently that something which she had locked up inside herself burst from its confines, shaking her with its violence as it swept through her.

'It's just sex,' she moaned, while the overhead spray lashed down, washing the tears down her face till she could taste the salt of them in her mouth. 'It's not love—and it's only because it's been so long. I'll hate myself—I'll hate you as well, afterwards.'

'Better to hate than feel nothing.' She felt the movement as he shrugged before he switched off the water and made a long arm to reach for a towel. 'Hate's only the other side of the coin. Every coin has two sides, and you can't have one without the other.' She felt the warmth of the towel about her and she was gently pushed out of the shower cubicle and on to the tiled floor of the bathroom to be rubbed dry and have her shower cap removed.

'M-my nightie!' she protested as Arkady draped her robe across her shoulders.

'You won't need it—or do you want me to behave like a Bulgar and tear it from your body?' She couldn't look up into his face, but she suspected he was laughing at her absurdity—and it was absurd for her to be behaving like this, only she couldn't get it out of her head that this was a different man from the husband she had known; that this wasn't the man she had married, made love with, borne his child. Or was this simply the other side of the coin called Arkady?

'Will that ease your conscience?' There was still laughter, a tiny thread of it, in his voice as he continued, 'If I'm rough with you so that when you wake in the morning, you can tell yourself it was none of your doing, that I'd violated you? No, Joanna, I shan't ill-treat you—that way, we'll both know the truth.'

Know the truth! She stifled an hysterical laugh with cold, shaking fingers against her quivering lips. Oh, she knew the truth very well, but only about herself. That for her there would never be another man—that even if she were free and finally found somebody she could live with, he would always and for ever be only second best.

'On your way,' he patted her bottom through the thin silk of her robe, and somehow the old

familiar gesture—he'd done it so often before—rid
her of her hysteria and loosened her tongue.

'Arkady,' she clasped the robe about her and
turned to face him, her grey eyes grave in a serious
face, 'it's hopeless, don't you see? I can't trust you
any more.' Unbidden, the thought of those two
figures in the garden came back to her, like a bit of
film printed indelibly on her mind—the way they
had melted together in the darkness as though they
had been made for each other. If he felt that sort
of love for another woman, she was sorry for
him—she knew what it was like; she felt that way
herself, and it was tearing her to pieces. If only he
would explain, bring it all out into the open,
maybe she could learn to live with it.

And live with it she would have to. Arkady
would never give up his son, never let her take
Dion away, just as she would never leave without
him! She watched as he shrugged himself into his
own short robe and came towards her, his tanned
feet and legs dark and strong against the white
tiles.

'You always talked too much,' he reproved, and
as she stumbled on her trailing sash, he gave a
little grunt of exasperation, swept her up in his
arms and carried her through to the bed.

It was well after nine o'clock when Joanna woke
to find herself alone in the bed—which was just as
well, she thought as she scrambled herself into a
sitting position, plumping up the pillows to form a
backrest. After all her protestations, her vows to
be uncooperative, her dour determination to lie
like a log and let things happen to her, to show
absolutely no feeling whatever—Arkady had won

the battle, and her response to his lovemaking had been uninhibited.

She blushed for herself, for the stupidly weak, female body whose need of him had been so stimulated that it had overpowered reason so that at last they had both fallen asleep, satiated and content. It wasn't a performance she was particularly proud of, especially her own part in it. Arkady had few scruples when it came to getting his own way, but she had prided herself on her own.

She had been feeling guilty ever since five o'clock in the morning when Dion had woken, demanding to be fed, and if it was true, the things she'd been told—that the state of a mother's mind could upset her baby's digestion—her son ought to have been writhing in agony for several hours if not all day, but Dion had done nothing of the sort. He had filled up and gone back to sleep in the crib without so much as a whimper.

Through the screens that opened on to the balcony she could see a clear, pale blue sky and feel the warmth of the day on her cheek, but the weather couldn't stay like this for much longer. It would never be really cold, but soon, in a week or two's time when November had come, heavy leaden clouds would darken the sky. Corfu had more than forty inches of rain per year, and nearly all of it fell in the short winter between December and the end of February.

It would be humid, of course, but healthy— what else could be expected of an island where the rainfall was so high and the vegetation so dense? Travel brochures said there were three and a half million olive trees alone on the island and nobody had ever bothered to count the other varieties—orange, lemon, cypress, plane and acacia. Most Corfiotes sniffed at those figures, saying the number of olive trees had been grossly underestimated, and Joanna was inclined to agree with them. Even here, on the top of the cliffs, they grew—sheltered by the fold in the ground and each one set in the old Moorish way on its own little terrace. Some of them so old that the gnarled and twisted trunks were little more than hollow shells.

Feet came clumping along the stone floor of the balcony, the screen doors were pushed open and Anna came in with a tray. Anna was old-fashioned—not for her the cotton dress, the pinny and a pair of sandals. Anna wore boots, sensible, lace-up black ones, under her nearly ankle-length black skirt, and her white apron was voluminous.

Her '*Kalimera*, Kyria Joanna,' was brief and she launched immediately into her slow, heavily accented English. 'The Kyrios Arkady has gone to Paxos, there is a note for you on the tray, and the Thespinis Kore has ridden on her scooter to Paleokastritsa.' She dumped the tray on Joanna's lap and glared at her accusingly from sharp little dark eyes. 'And I have not yet seen the baby!'

'*Efharisto*, and I'm sorry, *lipoome poli*,' Joanna's tongue stumbled over the words and most of her guilt was submerged in a desire to smooth down Anna's hackles, which were definitely up. She was a fierce old woman and easily hurt. When Anna was hurt, the food suffered, chicken came to the table nearly burned to a cinder and she only ever served Greek salad—chopped tomatoes.

'Kyrios Arkady spoke about Sylvie.' Joanna sought to create a diversion as she watched Anna swoop down on the crib and peel back Dion's coverings and prod him with a work-worn finger.

'Sylvie is a good girl,' Anna said absently as she examined the baby. 'A fine boy and big for his age, he will be tall, like Kyrios Arkady.'

'She's rather young.' Joanna was desperate to draw Anna's attention from the baby, she didn't want him woken before she'd sampled the coffee and the hot, napkin-wrapped roll in the tray. It was good to feel hungry once more—over the last year, she hadn't cared whether she ate or not. Anna replaced the cover and straightened to fix Joanna with dark, beady eyes.

'Sylvie knows more about babies than you do, *kyria*,' she admonished tartly. 'Hasn't she had the raising of the younger ones in her own family?' And her sniff showed how little she thought of her daughter-in-law's abilities. 'Her mother is a poor, sickly thing—Sylvie has done it all. When the Kyrios asked me this morning, I told him to call at the house on his way to Paleokastritsa. As soon as the girl arrives, I will bring her up to you. You will be risen by then.' And her glance told Joanna what Anna thought of young women who spent half of the morning in bed before she clumped out of the room.

And nobody had even mentioned Ilone— Joanna's brows crinkled into a frown. It was as if everybody was pretending Ilone wasn't there! Was this some ploy of Arkady's—to pretend something or somebody didn't exist? He must have known it was Ilone Joanna had meant when she had said she had seen them—there was nobody else it could have been. Or was it a kind of conspiracy— pretend Ilone isn't here and simple-minded Joanna will forget all about her?

Whatever it was, Ilone wasn't playing the same game. When, two hours later, Joanna went downstairs, leaving a sleeping Dion in the charge of a girl child who didn't look as though she had the strength to lift him, her *bête noir* was coming across the patio with a look on her face that meant she had something to say and was determined to say it.

'Joanna, my dear!' Ilone dropped smoothly and gracefully into a lounger and disposed of her secateurs and a trug of late roses on to a low table to take off her thick gardening gloves wearily. 'So much to do at this time of the year, the garden becomes a wilderness if it is neglected for even a day.'

Anna's boots came clumping through the doorway—dead on time. Joanna checked her watch—it was exactly eleven o'clock—and Anna banged a tray of coffee down on the low table at Joanna's elbow. She gave Ilone a curt nod and then concentrated her attention where she thought she might have the most trouble.

'You find Sylvie satisfactory, *kyria*?' Her very attitude dared Joanna to say 'no', and Joanna temporised.

'She's very small,' she said weakly, 'but she appears to know what to do, and Dion seems to like her. He certainly made no objection when she changed him.'

'There is no harm in being small.' Anna drew herself up indignantly to her full five foot no inches and glared. 'Sylvie must have aprons, *ne*? I will get them for her.'

Joanna weakened further, recalling the young girl's much washed, very faded and slightly undersized apparel—the fabric had looked as though it might fall to pieces if the slightest strain was put on it. But she had to be diplomatic; Anna would counter the slightest suggestion of charity with a burnt offering at dinner time.

'And some dresses.' She tried to look as though she had given it a lot of thought. 'Pink. I like the colour and it will suit her. You can get her one ready made one for now and we'll have the others made up when I've had a chance to look at some materials. I fancy a pink and white candy stripe.'

'Anna is getting too old for the work.' Ilone's voice came quietly but gratingly over the clump of Anna's triumphant retreat. 'And daily her cooking gets worse. Last night's dinner was a disaster, she had cooked the fish much too early, and if it hadn't been for the sauce, I doubt if we could have eaten it. Her way of showing her displeasure at having an extra guest, I suppose, and although I agreed with her sentiments—it was monstrous of Kore to produce an uninvited guest at such short notice—a beach boy! We can only hope the Apostolakis family don't ever hear of it. They could so easily disapprove of such behaviour. That Kore should be working is bad enough—in a hotel where she is exposed to all kinds of bad behaviour and ugly language from tourists—but this! We should have given him a glass of wine and shown him the door! Young girls like Kore have no discrimination, she should learn to be satisfied with the friends we choose for her—Serghios . . .'

'Have a cup of coffee and cool down,' Joanna advised sardonically as she seized the handle of the coffee pot and made herself remain seated when what she would have liked to have done was storm off back to her bedroom and remain there for the rest of the day. 'Kore's made it quite clear what she thinks of Serghios Apostolakis. She wouldn't have him as a gift, and since she's far too young to be thinking about marriage—too young to *be* married, I don't suppose Arkady would force her into anything. It's still only a tentative arrangement, surely?'

'But an arrangement.' Ilone's voice had the penetrating quality of a mosquito's whine and her lovely face had taken on an obstinate look. 'And Serghios will make her a good husband. She should be grateful that such an advantageous marriage has come her way. The Apostolakis family are very well connected—Serghios could have his pick from among the best of Athens society . . .'

'I wonder why he doesn't?' Joanna snapped tartly.

'. . . Whereas this American young man,' Ilone continued as though Joanna's interruption had never been—as if she hadn't spoken. 'He is too old for her and we know nothing about him. We do not even know whether he can afford to marry, whether he has sufficient money to keep Kore . . .'

'Oh, for pity's sake!' Joanna burst in indignantly. 'Can't you think of anything but marriage? I don't suppose Kore's even thought as far as that—it's just friendliness where she's concerned, and as for her inviting him here, surely that's better than meeting him behind our backs? She's at just the right age for secret assignations to have an appeal. So, to my way of thinking, telling her not to see him, forbidding her to invite him here, is all that's needed to make her more determined than ever.

We'd do better not to interfere—leave it to Arkady, she's his daughter, and he's quite capable of putting his foot down if she gets too much out of line.'

'I wish,' Ilone was acidly correct, 'I wish you would not use that dreadful slang of which you English are so fond. I can hardly understand your meaning, and as for leaving it all to Arkady, nowadays he thinks of nothing but his business and his son.' She shrugged elegantly. 'As soon as he discovered your child was a boy, nothing else mattered to him. He left immediately, saying he would bring the boy back with him—we hardly expected to see you, however.'

Joanna kept her head averted and her eyes firmly fixed on the horizon. Beyond the clifftops the sky was a clear blue, slightly darker than it had been earlier in the day, and through a break in the cliffs she could see the rim of the sea where it joined the sky—ink-dark, smooth, unruffled in the light breeze and gleaming in the sunlight.

'You mean the old "humiliation" thing, I suppose,' she made her voice light and carefree. 'I was supposed to cower away back in England, hide my head in shame and let him take my child away from me?'

'It would have been more dignified than forcing yourself on him once again.' Ilone's eyes held a feverish glitter. 'Some people have not yet made up their minds whether the child is truly Arkady's.'

Joanna flushed at the insult and felt her temper rising. 'They'll just have to wait and see, won't they?' she almost snarled before she recovered herself and became cool again. 'I don't think I care for this conversation, *thespinis*.' She put as much venom into that word as possible. Ilone's unmarried state was a running sore to the woman and she didn't like it emphasised. 'I suggest you think of something different to talk about,' she continued smoothly.

'Oh no.' Ilone had found Joanna's weak spot and intended to hammer away at it unmercifully. 'There is such a lot of talk in a small place like this, and it isn't good for Arkady. He's the one I'm thinking about—and, of course, Kore. Your being here could do incalculable harm to her marriage prospects. The Apostolakis could withdraw their offer just for that reason alone. A stepmother who actively encouraged a young girl to behave indiscreetly . . .'

'Back to Kore again,' Joanna sighed resignedly, but inwardly she was relieved. Her stepdaughter was such a nice safe subject. 'Please remember that it was Arkady who said she could take a job if she could find one, and I don't think anything she does, short of running away with another man, would put them off. Her *prika*, her dowry, would keep their spotty son in style for the rest of his life. Good American dollars, a legacy from her grandmother, I believe, and all sitting in the bank and earning interest until she's eighteen!' Joanna would have liked to borrow an oft-heard phrase from her late aunt in Bedford and say 'Put that on your needles and knit it!' but caution gained the upper hand. Instead, she threw down a challenge.

'As far as I'm concerned, Kore may invite any of her friends here—male or female, I don't give a hoot, and they'll all be made welcome.'

'But only until you leave,' Ilone spat out like a small black Persian kitten. 'After the child no longer needs you, Arkady will send you away.'

'Like hell he will!' Joanna's anger flared again. 'That's my child upstairs, mine as well as Arkady's, and if you think I'm going to leave him to your tender, loving care, you've got another think coming! I'll see us both dead before I do that—and you needn't bother to tell Arkady I've been rude to you, I'll tell him myself!' And, still carrying her coffee cup, she stalked away along the patio in the direction of the outside staircase which led directly to the balcony.

In the bedroom, she halted. Dion was asleep and Sylvie was busy sorting his clothes. The girl had been busy; everything was spick and span, discarded clothing had been taken away somewhere and the bed looked as though it had come straight from an exhibition. There wasn't a wrinkle to be seen. Joanna forced a smile to her face and marched through to the bathroom, where again chaos had been restored to order, and she closed the door behind her quietly instead of slamming it as she very much wanted to do.

The mirror gave back a reflection which was nearer to the Joanna of a year ago. There was quite a becoming flush on her usually pale cheeks and her eyes were bright once more, but it was only the remains of temper, and as she watched, the flush paled away and the grey of her eyes darkened to dullness. Being defiant was all very well if one had the necessary clout to back it up, and she hadn't!

She knew only too well she was here on sufferance, that it was only because of Dion that she wasn't rotting away into old age in England. Arkady's lovemaking meant nothing except that he was a virile man, she was willing and they were good together in bed. She licked lips gone dry with fear and swallowed at the bitter lump that was stuck in her throat, sipping at Anna's strong, sweet coffee to wash away the taste of defeat.

It was all very well to know her husband didn't love her, that he was only making use of her for just as long as she was necessary to Dion—but she didn't want it rammed down her throat!

CHAPTER FIVE

THE beach buggy was quite the nicest, easiest thing to drive, Joanna decided as she tootled along the track from the villa to Krini. The springing might be almost non-existent, but the big, soft tyres gave the little vehicle a good purchase on the rough ground and they ironed out a lot of the bumps and jars of badly surfaced roads. She wrinkled her nose at the thought of the minor road from Krini to Paleokastritsa, a long succession of repairs and places in need of repair, and so narrow. It was all right for Arkady to bounce the Range Rover along it, but for her, she preferred something smaller and narrower so she didn't have to reverse every time she met an oncoming car.

Outside the taverna at Makredes there was the usual table and the usual group of four or five elderly men playing cards and making a bottle of retsina between them last all afternoon while they puffed at their strong, odd-tasting Greek cigarettes and kept an eye on a parcel of infants who were playing under the table. Joanna slowed down as she came up to them; the street was narrow and the little ones, unused to traffic in this village which was the end of the line, moved like quicksilver— far too quickly for the elderly men to catch them.

At Lakones, Joanna received a courteous greeting from a priest in the traditional stovepipe hat—it might have been accompanied by a smile, but she couldn't tell through his luxuriant beard.

Or what she had taken for a greeting could have been him sending up a swift prayer for a quick and painless death as she swerved in the narrow street to avoid a stately cockerel who thought he owned the place.

The hairpin bends from Lakones down to the campsite where she would join the main road to Paleokastritsa occupied all her attention and gave her no time for thought, although almost any road in Corfu made her concentrate so that she hardly ever saw much of the scenery. She swooped past the two places where tourists were advised to stop and contemplate the view, but that wasn't altogether because she was an indifferent driver. Today she hadn't the time to spare; she was meeting Arkady who had been overseeing his villas on Paxos for the last week, and she wanted to be on time.

Almost a month had passed since he had brought her and Dion to Corfu—four weeks of warm but gentle sunshine with only the occasional short, sharp burst of rain, and although they hadn't been weeks of unalloyed bliss, she had been quite happy. A fussy Fiat overtook her, blaring frantically because she'd wandered into the middle of the road, so she put her reminiscing on one side for the moment and concentrated on getting down to the marina in one piece. If Arkady was a bit late, she would find herself somewhere to sit and have a good think about her situation.

The cabin cruiser wasn't tied up to its buoy—it wasn't even in sight, so she parked the buggy outside a seafront taverna, slipped a cardigan about her shoulders and padded off down to an old wooden jetty, to sit on the side with her legs

dangling while she kept an eye on the southern
horn of the narrow bay—the direction from which
her husband would be coming.

Her husband—Joanna frowned fearfully. Since
that first night in the villa, he hadn't touched her,
hadn't seemed to want to; not once! He had slept
on the narrow bed in the little dressing-room, but
he hadn't been at home all that much. She had
found herself missing him, and a three-cornered
fight seemed to develop between herself, Ilone and
Anna—all Anna's fault, although she really
couldn't be blamed. As Anna said, loudly and
often, she took her orders from the Kyria Joanna,
so Ilone's smallest request had to be the subject of
consultation, and if the result of the confab didn't
agree with Anna—or vice versa—the old woman
took it out on the food.

Joanna couldn't even excuse herself and be
absent from the frequent arguments. She had no
excuse. Sylvie had taken over the baby and his
mother was only expected to put in an appearance
when he yelled for food! Joanna felt her forehead
dampen with nervous perspiration—she was being
gently but surely eased out. In another few
months, Dion would be weaned, and what then?
She didn't know, and she didn't dare speculate.

Deep in thought, she missed the boat coming
into sight, and when she looked it was already
there and Arkady was warping the stern line on to
the mooring buoy. Joanna watched the flash of his
brown limbs as he heaved the anchor over the
bows and then adjusted the stern lines before he
dived overboard and was swimming strongly
towards her, the sea plastering his hair into a
smooth black cap on his head. Automatically she

dived into her shoulder bag for the towel and dry tee-shirt she had brought for him; he could hardly drive back to the villa in just a pair of white trunks.

'*Gineka mou!*' Arkady reached up a brown hand, hauled himself lithely on to the sunwarmed old boards of the landing stage and shook himself like a terrier, spattering salt water droplets in all directions before he reached for her hand to take it lightly in his own. 'How is my son?'

'Very well,' said said sedately, proffering the towel and tee-shirt. This was, after all, Greece, and one didn't make a show of emotion in public. Some long-buried humour rose in her so that she smiled. 'You've only been away a week, so he hasn't learned to walk yet!'

'And the rest of the family?' He walked barefoot beside her, struggling his still damp body into the tee-shirt before he rubbed his hair with the towel.

'Kore is busy.' Joanna detailed off the small happenings of the week. 'Her hotel has a fresh batch of winter tourists—all English, so she's been co-opted as a guide on the little tours arranged for them. Dion seems to have a bit of a chill, he whinges and snuffles a bit—Anna thinks it might be a tooth and he'll be a bit fretful for a while, although I think it's a bit early for anything like that. Hank Sommers came to dinner last evening, but you weren't there, so Anna disapproved—she burned the pork chops and,' she saved the best— or worst, depending on which way one looked at it—until last, 'and Ilone flew out to Athens yesterday morning.'

'So you and Kore dined with the water-skiing instructor unchaperoned?' They had reached the

buggy and Arkady handed her into the passenger
seat, climbed behind the steering wheel and turned
to her, one black eyebrow cocked. Joanna
remained calm, she even managed a bit of sardonic
humour.

'If you could call it that,' she shrugged. 'I
wouldn't, myself. Anna had Sylvie serve dinner on
the patio while she stood under one of the arches
like a black and white-clad Witch of Endor with
overtones of Cassandra—muttering! Don't ask me
what she was muttering, it was all in Greek, but it
sounded doom-laden and vitriolic enough to have
been a prophecy or an incantation. She definitely
didn't approve, because she scorched the pork
chops, and after dinner she went off to the kitchen,
I think to stick pins in a wax image of him! One
thing I do know, though, Kore's going off him, as
I said she would, but she trotted out some
beautiful manners, so it didn't show—much!'

Arkady chuckled. 'And aren't you going to say
"I told you so" and put your tongue out at me?'

Joanna lifted her nose and looked down it,
being superior. 'I'm not that badly mannered,' she
told him smugly, while her brain raced ahead.
Hank had always been well behaved, but . . . The
oftener she met him, talked with him, the uneasier
she had become. For one thing, despite his
ingenuous manner and his appearance of youth, she
suspected he was much older than she had thought
at first. And Ilone had confirmed that suspicion—
nobody could kid Ilone, she was far too sharp and
her eyes saw everything. And another thing—
Joanna supposed it was what had started her
suspicions. Hank had said he used a Rolliecon to
take snaps, but that didn't add up. A Rolliecon

wasn't the sort of camera one used to take snaps—
it was bulky and heavy to carry about, there were
only twelve exposures on the reel of paperbacked
film it held, and it wasn't the easiest camera to
focus when it was hand-held.

She shook her head to rid it of the fantastic
ideas that were swimming through it and forced
herself to pay attention as Arkady spoke.

'And who's the new boy-friend? I suppose there
is one?'

Jo felt her jaw drop with surprise. 'You'd allow
it? I thought Kore's future was all mapped out—
only girl friends from here on in.'

'Could I stop it?' His dark eyes slanted down at
her mockingly and the quality of his smile rid her
of the last of her fantasies. It was only because her
stepdaughter was so young—what an excuse to
build up something on mere supposition and with
nothing concrete to back it up—she was getting as
bad as Ilone, only willing to think the worst of
people.

'Well,' she had brightened up considerably. 'I'm
not sure, but I think it might be the son of the
couple who've taken the villa near Pagi. They're a
Greek family from England, aren't they? Didn't
you say they had some restaurants in London?
The boy's about eighteen or nineteen, and Kore
skipped a proper breakfast to whizz over there
early this morning on her scooter with a boxful of
electric light bulbs.'

'Greater love hath no man,' quoted Arkady with
a chuckle. 'I hope she didn't break too many of
them. There's a road of sorts from Vistonas to
Pagi, but it's unsurfaced.'

'And the Apostolakis family?' Joanna kept her

eyes on her clasped hands. 'Will there be trouble from that quarter, do you think? Would they be likely to cancel the arrangement? You see, Kore's so lively, she's finding her feet, and she's very strong-willed . . .'

'Gineka mou,' one of his hands left the steering wheel and came to pat her admonishingly, 'look after your baby and your household and leave me to deal with my daughter. Is that all that's happened while I've been away?'

'Almost.' Joanna debated with herself and decided to tell a part of the truth. 'I made a brief trip to Corfu—I beg your pardon, I should have said Kerkira. Shopping, you know, but I couldn't do much, only having four hours free is limiting.' She said nothing of her visit to the British Consulate office or of the smooth young man who had assured her that yes, she was right, her son had dual nationality, all that was needed was his father's written permission and Dion could accompany his mother to China, if that was where she wanted to go. Joanna had smiled sweetly as she'd thanked the unhelpful creature and walked away into the Spianada, supposed to be the largest and most beautiful square in all Greece, but its grace and beauty were lost on her.

Later she had wandered into another square, smaller and less élite, to stop at a café and stare miserably down at the coffee she had ordered. What was the use of even trying when everything was against her? She didn't even have her own passport, Arkady had taken charge of it when they had arrived here from Athens and she hadn't seen it since—and he certainly wouldn't give written permission for her to take Dion anywhere!

The memory of that afternoon took all the peace out of her soul. Slowly, as she had stirred in more and more sugar, making the coffee well nigh undrinkable, her misery had resolved itself into resentment. Why should it be so easy for some and so difficult for others? Memories of newspaper headlines had come to mind—British children kidnapped from their English mothers by foreign fathers and smuggled out of Britain—taken out for a supposed ride in a car which was supposed to be just for a few hours, and the children and their fathers had vanished to pop up in France, Iraq, all sorts of countries, and they had all travelled without a shred of documentation.

The foreign fathers must have had some help, so why had the British Consulate to be so stuffy and go by the book? It wasn't fair! Joanna found herself almost wishing that Dion had been a girl; Arkady would not have wanted him—her—it then. Girls were too expensive, men had to be paid to marry them; at least, in Greece they did!

It had taken Joanna all of two days to get over that resentment, to accept what seemed the inevitable, and even that she did with a bad grace, determined to be as awkward as possible as often as possible—yet here she was, meekly rushing around, collecting her husband, carrying on innocuous conversations with him, making a show of being the subservient Greek wife—and only because if she didn't, she stood to lose Dion for ever!

She made no hurry about getting ready for dinner. She fed her son at seven o'clock and took her time about it, and tried to ignore Arkady as he passed to and fro, on his way to the bathroom and back, as he flipped through the contents of his half of the wardrobe, and she turned her back on him while he dressed and fiddled with his hair to bring some order into the tangle of curls left by the shower.

'You'll be late, and Anna has moussaka,' he told her when, ready, he came to stand and watch.

'It's Saturday, Anna always has moussaka on Saturday,' she snapped tartly. 'It's about the only thing she doesn't burn, not even when she's upset. Anyway, Dion comes first.' She gave him an angry glare. 'Or do you want me to have to leave the table halfway through a meal because he's yelling the place down?'

'Don't be a fool, Joanna, and stop thinking I'm one as well,' he snapped back at her. 'You can hurry when it suits you. Apparently tonight it doesn't suit, for some peculiar reason of your own. You're deliberately going at a snail's pace. You finished feeding him a good ten minutes ago and you've just sat and cuddled him ever since.'

'He likes being cuddled,' she protested angrily. 'Babies need more than food, you know, they need love. Why, in prehistoric times, a child was never out of its mother's arms.'

'You say the most ridiculous things,' Arkady snorted softly. 'That wasn't so much love as a desire to protect the species. Put him into his crib, dress yourself and come down for a meal.'

'Your father's in a bossy mood, but when isn't he?' said Joanna to a sleeping Dion, 'and he doesn't care that you've got a bit of a cold and your chest sounds as though it's full of dried leaves. He doesn't realise . . .'

'I realise you're deliberately procrastinating.' He

laid a hand on her shoulder and shook her gently. 'What's the matter, *karthia*? Are you afraid of a possible tête-à-tête? You needn't be—Kore's there already, can't you hear the hi-fi going full•blast? There can't be anything much wrong with the boy if he can sleep through that row. *Hurry!*'

Reluctantly, Joanna laid the baby down, very carefully so as not to wake him, and then straightened up to nibble thoughtfully at a fingernail.

'Now, what to wear?' she mused aloud. 'Satin and my tiara or jeàns and a sweat-shirt? I know, I'll have a shower while I make up my mind— Oh, go *on*!' she added snappishly. 'I won't be long behind you.' But as the door closed behind him, she felt like weeping. Arkady had been in a good mood, and now she'd probably spoiled it—why did she have this destructive impulse to ruin things time and time again? If only she'd never learned the truth about him, she could have been supremely happy living in her fool's paradise.

Nevertheless, when she went into the lounge-cum-dining-room, she looked calm enough—or so her mirror told her. It told her a few other things as well, that she was putting on a little weight, much needed and quite flattering—that already her hair was looking better. It hadn't quite regained its colour, but the rosy apricot gold was coming back, and the soft tan on her arms and legs was very becoming when teamed up with a sleeveless white linen dress and white high-heeled sandals—and her eyes were brighter as well. So much so that she had treated them to a little eye-shadow and mascaraed her long lashes. Having done that, it seemed a pity not to continue, so her cheeks had a soft flush, mostly out of a box, and her mouth was a tender deep pink against the pallor of her skin.

Arkady turned at her entrance and there was a warm, very appreciative glow in his eyes as they rested on her, taking in everything, the rounding of her hips, her long slender legs which didn't look quite so sticklike, even the dimple which, for the past year, had been only a crease in her thin cheek. He held up a decanter.

'An aperitif, darling?' Somehow the trite, overworked English endearment sounded more meaningful when it came from his lips, and Joanna had to steel herself to show no answering pleasure.

'Not that,' she shook her head. 'Tonic or soda water, please. Dion doesn't like it when I drink alcohol. He glares at me.' Out of the corner of her eye, she caught Kore's scowl as the girl looked up from the magazine she was flicking through. Arkady's daughter was a bundle of contradictions—one minute as nice as pie, helpful and pleasant, and the next, sunk into the sullens with not a friendly word to be had from her. She'd been so pleased, so happy the day Joanna had arrived, but it hadn't lasted long, and now the pleasant relationship had gone to pot.

There was nothing overtly obvious, of course, but Joanna could feel the lack of response and she had attempted to shrug it off, enduring what couldn't be dismissed as thoughtlessness. Kore was probably suffering from the remains of a guilty conscience—not all the time, only when she remembered about a particular beach hut and a boat boy called Stephanos—and perhaps one other thing, But gradually it was bound to wear off, or so Joanna assured herself. It would take time for Kore to realise her little secrets were quite safe with her new stepmother.

Joanna wished there was some way she could think of to reassure the girl; it was a pity that between them they couldn't drag it all out in the open, get it off their chests—bare their breasts. Her lips curved into a smile at the old-fashioned phrase, yet it was so appropriate, it conjured up just the right picture. But she knew she couldn't really expect anything like that. Teenagers were so sensitive and prickly, especially with somebody who knew about a happening of which they weren't very proud, which showed them in the worst possible light.

Joanna followed a clear fresh vegetable soup with moussaka and became immersed in it. It was very, very good and not a bit charred, which said a lot for the state of Anna's temper. Gradually she started missing bits of the conversation between Arkady and his daughter, and by the time she was part way through her second helping, she was missing it all. Feeding a baby with an appetite as big as Dion's was a hunger-making exercise in itself, and when Anna was in a good temper the food she produced was so delicious it had to be treated with the respect it deserved. Nothing less than total concentration would do, so Kore's high-pitched squawk of wrath and her, 'You're going to Athens and without *me*!' was an intrusive thing and spoiled the remains of the second helping completely. Joanna paused with a forkful poised to put in her mouth and raised her head to pay attention.

'*We* are going to Athens.' That was Arkady

being flatly determined. 'Joanna, myself, and of course, Dion. Maybe we'll take Sylvie, that's something for Joanna to decide. It's dryer there, not so humid, and Joanna's worried about Dion's chest—she says it sounds as though it's full of dry leaves. We shall be back in time for Christmas.'

'Why Sylvie?' demanded Kore aggressively. 'Why not me? I can do anything Sylvie can do and it'd give me a chance to do a bit of shopping. I've earned quite a lot of money, tips and things, and what's the good of it here? Everything's geared for the tourist trade, all the shops have the same things, there's nothing different! Besides, Anna's always complaining that she doesn't get a chance to clean the place properly. If I went with you, she'd have Sylvie to help her . . .'

'A good point.' Joanna approved of his manner to Kore; very reasonable, very adult. 'But it depends on two things—firstly Joanna. Does she consider you to be a suitable stand-in for Sylvie, and secondly, what about your job? You bullied until I gave permission for you to take it.'

'I can take a short holiday, can't I?' Kore was fighting to get her own way, her head up, her chin firm and a determined glow in her long dark eyes. 'I've been working non-stop ever since April—and there won't be any problem about taking up where I left off when we come back. I'm too useful. The hotel manager was only saying yesterday that I'm the best receptionist they've ever had. I was going to ask for some time off anyway now things have gone quiet for the winter.'

'Joanna,' Arkady touched her hand where it lay on the table and she pretended to come out of her dream, dropping her forkful of food back on to her plate with a clatter. She had felt like throwing it down, but that wouldn't have done—it might have betrayed the fact she was seething with anger. Athens! Ilone was in Athens! Lord, couldn't he do without the sight of the woman for more than a week? Did he have to trail in her wake everywhere?

'Hmm? Sorry, I wasn't listening.' But as she said it, she knew Arkady wasn't deceived. He knew very well she had heard Kore's protest, she would have had to be deaf not to—she must be as transparent as glass.

'We are going to Athens,' but he explained as though he had believed her and he wasn't asking if it was what she wanted, just telling her what he had decided. 'And Kore wants to know if she may come with us in Sylvie's place.'

'Anything Sylvie can do, I can do, and Dion likes me.' Kore was daring her to object and Joanna heard herself being weak.

'Sounds all right to me.'

'Good,' Arkady nodded as if it was all settled— which it was, in his mind. 'We'll stay at Ilone's house, I'll ask her for the keys when she gets back tomorrow,' and as Joanna raised a surprised eyebrow, 'Didn't you know she was returning so soon? She only went to get her hair done.'

'Now how could I be expected to know a thing like that?' she muttered sarcastically, hoping Kore wouldn't hear. 'My mind balks at the expense of a hairdo that includes the air fare.' Along the length of the table she could feel the force of Kore's repressed wishes, and she wondered comically if this was how God felt when he heard some silent but particularly fervent prayer.

'Of course Kore may come.' This time she didn't mutter, it came out clearly and emphatically. 'She'll be perfect, she knows Athens; and if you'll be a bit co-operative and do a bit of baby-sitting, she'll be able to show me where all the best shops are.'

'You plan to spend a lot of money?' Arkady raised an eyebrow.

'No.' She edged the remains of the moussaka on her plate on to her fork and conveyed it to her mouth, where she chewed it with a thoughtful expression on her face, and when her mouth was empty she leaned back with a sigh of satisfaction. 'No more than you can afford, a few things for Dion and some Christmas presents.' She left the sting till the last, bringing it out softly and triumphantly. 'I've got a little money left, I shall give you a cheque to cover anything I spend on myself.' And with a great deal of satisfaction she watched the anger glow in his eyes, his nostrils thin and his mouth tighten into a hard, straight line.

The couple of hours after dinner was over were easy. Kore had a stack of video films, and as her taste ran to action, horror and space adventures, they sat through a full-length space epic, very noisy and to Joanna quite incomprehensible, but she used the darkness and the time to think and fume.

How dared Arkady install her in a house he and Ilone had used as a love nest on their trips to Athens! As far as she was concerned, it only went to show how few principles he had. She couldn't think of anything more degrading.

Arkady came into the bedroom just as she was

restoring Dion to his crib and tucking the covers about him.

'Hush!' she ordered peremptorily. 'He's still fretful and it's taken me ages to get him off to sleep. Don't you dare make a noise!'

'All your consideration for our son and none for me, *gineka mou*.' He was frowning and his dark eyes rested broodingly on her face. 'I think you've become that worst of things, an obsessive mother with not a thought in your head for anybody or anything but your child.'

'Dion's my son, my baby,' she spat at him, but very softly, her eyes never leaving the infant's sleeping face. 'He's the reason I'm here, isn't he? I can't think of any other. You don't love me and I don't . . .'

'. . . But you told a different story the first night we arrived here,' he reminded her, equally softly. 'Not in words, of course, but, as you English say, actions speak louder than words.'

Joanna flushed, grabbed at a little false sophistication and shrugged airily while her eyes dulled to a dark, stormy grey in her face from which the flush had faded so that it became almost paper-white.

'Oh, that night,' she made it sound of no consequence. 'I told you why, or didn't I? I certainly meant to—although with your wealth of experience, you shouldn't have needed telling. It had been a long time, and unlike you, I didn't, still don't go in for extra-marital relationships. Perhaps if I had, you wouldn't have found me so easy.' She lifted her chin defiantly. 'I'll see I don't get into that state again, though,' she added hardily.

For a moment she thought he was going to hit

her, he certainly looked mad enough, but suddenly all the rage was gone from his face to be replaced with sardonic amusement.

'And how do you propose to go about that, my dear? You've just said you don't make extra-marital arrangements and I've no intention of divorcing you. Are you going to break a habit of a lifetime and take a lover, or are you set on vows of chastity? You're—how old? Twenty-five? The rest of your life is going to last a long, long time, and I don't think you could hold out for ever against a determined man.'

'Do you mind changing the subject?' she suggested aloofly, turning her back on him. 'I don't think I care for this conversation.'

'But I do!' His hands on her shoulders turned her about to face him. 'We'll settle this now ...'

'No, we won't!' It was useless to struggle against those hands, they were far too powerful for her small strength, so she stood very still and glared at him stonily. 'Not your way, Arkady. I'm here because of Dion. I didn't ask to come, I didn't want to, and I fully understand that when I'm no longer required, I shall be sent home.' She made one of her instant decisions, the kind she always found herself regretting, as when she had agreed to marry him—but she could no longer help herself. 'You married me to get a son—well, you've got him, but,' she raised her chin gallantly, 'I shall do everything in my power to take him back with me when I go. I'll lie and cheat if I have to, but I'll try! And now, if you don't mind, I'm very tired ...'

She wasn't just tired, she was exhausted, and probably looked it, she thought ruefully. Tired to death and as plain as a pikestaff—and she shouldn't have warned Arkady of her intentions. He would now be on his guard, which would make everything just that much more difficult. But it was too late now—as it always was—for regrets. Wearily, she drew back the covers and slid herself between the sheets, turning away from him to bury her face in the pillow.

She felt as miserable now as she had done after Dion was born, a sort of weary hopelessness which the doctors had brushed aside as postnatal depression, and it was no use wishing, 'If only'. That only made it worse.

'I think we kill each other a little every day,' Arkady's voice came softly as he switched off the light and slid into bed beside her, yet not touching her, and she found herself almost crying at the sadness in his voice. She lay there in the darkness, curled up into as small a ball as possible, cold and unhappy, until at last she could no longer hold back her tears. They pricked painfully behind her eyelids, gathered, spilled over and ran down her face to soak into her pillow. There were no sobs, it was as though a tiny dam had broken, and when she had cried herself out, she fell asleep with the taste of her tears in her mouth.

Some time in the damp, grey light of the false dawn, Joanna stirred, half opening her eyes and then settling back into sleepy comfort. The tears she had shed must have acted as a safety valve— she felt as though she had wept away her hurt and bitterness, and the depression was gone. One day at a time from now on—no yesterdays, no tomorrows, because the one was better forgotten and the other didn't bear thinking about.

She knew at that moment that her future was

sealed tight. If Arkady wouldn't let Dion go, then she would stay with him; she would insist on it. He wasn't a cruel man, it wasn't his fault that his love for her—and he did love her in his way—was less than the older, deeper love that bound him. Oh lord! Joanna smiled wryly to herself, she was beginning to think like a high-flown romantic novel—the kind spinsters wept over!

Some time during the night she must have uncurled herself from her icy isolation; the warmth of Arkady was against her and she could feel the weight of his arm across her body. Her wry smile became rueful. When the brain stopped working, the senses took over—if she turned, she would see his face, and he always had looked younger, more vulnerable when he was asleep. It was a temptation, but she resisted it—Dion wasn't awake and demanding yet, she had at least another hour before the baby woke. She closed her eyes and relaxed to feel the heavy, warm arm tighten about her waist.

It felt very, very good!

TO EXPERIENCE A WORLD OF ROMANCE.

How to Enter Sweepstakes & How to get 4 FREE BOOKS, A FREE TOTE BAG and A BONUS MYSTERY GIFT.

1. Check ONLY ONE OPTION BELOW.
2. Detach Official Entry Form and affix proper postage.
3. Mail Sweepstakes Entry Form before the deadline date in the rules.

H·A·R·L·E·Q·U·I·N

FIRST·CLASS

Sweepstakes

OFFICIAL ENTRY FORM

Check one:

☐ Yes. Enter me in the Harlequin First Class Sweepstakes and send me 4 FREE HARLEQUIN ROMANCE® novels plus a FREE Tote Bag and a BONUS Mystery Gift. Then send me 6 brand new HARLEQUIN ROMANCE® novels every month as they come off the presses. Bill me at the low price of $1.65 each (a savings of $0.30 off the retail price). There are no shipping, handling or other hidden charges. I understand that the 4 Free Books, Tote Bag and Mystery Gift are mine to keep with <u>no obligation to buy</u>.

☐ No. I don't want to receive the Four Free HARLEQUIN ROMANCE® novels, a Free Tote Bag and a Bonus Gift. However, I <u>do</u> wish to enter the sweepstakes. Please notify me if I win.

See back of book for official rules and regulations.
Detach, affix postage and mail Official Entry Form today!

116-CIR-EAXR

FIRST NAME_____ LAST NAME_____
(Please Print)

ADDRESS_____ APT._____

CITY_____

PROV./STATE_____ POSTAL CODE/ZIP_____
"Subscription Offer limited to one per household and not valid to current Harlequin Romance® subscribers. Prices subject to change."

ENTER THE H•A•R•L•E•Q•U•I•N
FIRST•CLASS *Sweepstakes*

Detach, Affix Postage and Mail Today!

Harlequin First Class Sweepstakes
P.O. Box 52010
Phoenix, AZ 85072-9987

Put stamp here.
The Post Office
will not
deliver mail
without postage.

CHAPTER SIX

'IF you don't care to go to Athens, we could go to Rhodes. I also have some business there.' Arkady helped himself to a cup of tea from Joanna's tray and sat himself on the side of the bed. 'Have you any preference?'

'You couldn't find some business in Gibraltar, I suppose?' Joanna sipped at her cup and marvelled how much better she felt—quite well enough to make this into a kind of game.

Arkady snorted with laughter. 'I could, but I won't,' he said with relish. 'I refuse to take you anywhere you can wave your pretty passport under your national flag. I don't trust you, *gineka mou*, you will try to steal my son away from me. I sometimes think you forget he's my son as well as yours. He needs you now, but later on he will need me—it is altogether too much for a woman to be mother and father to her child.'

'You've got a point there,' Joanna sighed in mock regret. 'I don't know a thing about football or cricket. But,' she wrinkled her brows as she looked at him over the rim of her teacup, 'lots of women have to do just that, manage on their own. Your own mother . . . you told me once that your father died when you were a baby and that your mother . . .'

'Did the best she could, but she often wished my father had lived. She said so. Often, I think, to give me the hidings I so richly deserved—my mother could never catch me! And I missed him, although I never knew him—there are some things a boy can only say to his father.' Arkady smiled at her with a rueful grimace mixed up in the curve of his mouth and squeezed her hand where it lay on the bedspread.

'Another thing,' he said so gently that the implication didn't strike her all at once, it was delayed until he had stopped talking. 'I would like Dion to have a brother or a sister soon—only children can be very lonely, I remember being so, and I think the gap between our children should be as short as possible, no more than two years. In that way the elder doesn't see the younger as a rival or an intruder.'

Joanna concealed her gasp with a cough and looked down at their hands, his strong and brown with exposure and hers smaller and pale by comparison. 'For that,' she muttered, 'you need co-operation, and,' when he didn't answer immediately, she went on with a show of defiance, 'I don't think I could offer you that. It all sounds very cold-blooded to me.'

'Cold-blooded?' he smiled again—Joanna thought it looked more like a smirk. 'Oh no, *agape*. I can assure you there will be nothing like that about it, and for proof . . .' He swooped over her, abandoning her hand to hold her face between his palms while his mouth found hers, stifling her protest.

Crazy things affected her, the smell of his aftershave, the feel of his lips as they gently but firmly parted her own, the cool touch of his skin against hers which seemed to be very heated by comparison. She felt the beat of his heart against her breast, getting muddled with her own which was hammering violently as something hot and insistent broke loose inside her, swamping her, drugging her into pleasure. There was no room left in her for thought, only for feeling, the crispness of his hair as she threaded her fingers through it, the scorch of his fingers as they trailed from her cheeks down her throat, the bitter sweetness that filled her when they caressed her breast, brushing aside the thin stuff of her nightdress. She didn't even hear the door being flung open, and it was only Kore's high voice, almost strident with disappointment, which brought her back to the present.

'Why aren't you going to Athens?'

Arkady recovered much more quickly; Joanna nearly wept at the realisation. Herself, she felt as though she had to swim up to the surface from a great depth, but he was there already, pulling her nightdress back to cover her, straightening the bedclothes and being upright and cool all in one swift movement.

'What, about Athens?' He wasn't even breathing hard.

'I've just seen Anna.' Kore's small face was tight with disappointment. 'She says you told her you mightn't be going there after all. Papa, you promised . . .'

'My fault.' Joanna struggled for command over her voice, which showed signs of wobbling throatily. 'I was trying to talk your papa into taking us to Gibraltar instead. I've never been there, never even seen it, but your papa says he has no business in Gibraltar, so it has to be either Athens or Rhodes. Which do you prefer?'

'Athens.' Kore was prompt, too prompt. Joanna had the idea her stepdaughter didn't care where she went as long as she went somewhere, but who could blame her? She had worked very hard since April, the girl was probably at the end of her tether—coping with tourists wasn't a job Joanna would have fancied for herself. The pay wasn't high and the constant ironing out of little difficulties would be shattering.

'We *are* going?' Kore demanded.

'Yes,' Arkady said curtly, 'and kindly knock at a bedroom door in future before you storm in.'

'I did!' His daughter was indignant, throwing the words over her shoulder as she stormed back out and hurried off down the stairs.

'So you see, *agape*,' Arkady continued as though they hadn't been interrupted, 'there will be no cold-bloodedness—I don't think that's possible between us. It's still there, this thing we have, but,' as he watched Joanna's face tighten into a chill aloofness, 'we won't rush it. We'll start again, right back at the beginning.'

It was a reprieve, and she watched him disappear through the door, carrying the tea-tray. It would be so easy to agree, to say yes, but like a child badly burned by fire, she was wary, afraid to go near it in case she was burned again. She hadn't healed completely from the last burning. Would he understand if she tried to explain?

With a glance at her watch, a quick look in the crib at the sleeping baby and a moan of distress, she jumped out of bed. Sylvie would be here soon, it was nearly nine o'clock, and downstairs Anna would have laid out hot fresh rolls and coffee, and if she didn't hurry—Kore had a tremendous appetite. She showered swiftly, hurried herself into a pair of jeans and a tee-shirt, flung a light cardigan about her shoulders against the cool of the morning, gave her hair a swift brushing but leaving it loose and hurried downstairs.

Ilone arrived back just before lunch with a sweet smile and a kiss for Kore, a 'I-hope-you've-missed-me-as-much-as-I've-missed-you' look for Arkady and a brief nod in Joanna's direction—and her hair didn't look a bit different!

She hurried off to her room, dismissing Kore's chatter with a wry, 'I must change, dear. One gets so filthy travelling nowadays. Tell me all about it over lunch,' which Kore did.

'Papa's taking Jo and Dion to Athens—he has some business there, and Jo says that I can go with them instead of Sylvie.'

'Oh! How very inconvenient,' Ilone was smooth as cream. 'I met the Apostolakis family while I was there, they took me out to dinner, and I returned the compliment by asking them here for dinner one night this week. If your papa intends to be away longer than a couple of days, I'd advise you to let Sylvie go with them. It won't be much fun for you, dear—babysitting all the time while your papa is busy and Joanna does the usual round of sightseeing. I suppose you haven't thought of that.'

'It's not going to be like that!' Kore was angrily defiant, and Joanna looked sideways at her in surprise. Her stepdaughter's temper seemed to be on a very short rein nowadays. 'It isn't, is it, Joanna?' Kore demanded fiercely.

Joanna, who had finished her grilled red mullet and pushed her plate aside, was occupied in slicing grapes into her dish of home-made yoghurt and took her time about replying.

'No, it isn't,' she said calmly, and gave her husband a swift glance. 'Actually, your father's going to be doing most of the babysitting, and as for sightseeing, this will be far from the first time I've been to Athens, so I don't need a guided tour. It's the shopping we're going for, and who wants a man for that? They don't have enough patience.'

'I have a lot of patience,' Arkady broke in with a meaningful glance at his wife, and Joanna felt a faint flush creep into her cheeks as she caught the look in his dark eyes. 'But I admit it wears thin when women can't make up their minds about which article they want to buy after they've turned over all the stock in the shop. Given a choice, women dither.' He pursed his lips and his voice was a falsetto caricature of a woman dithering. 'I like the red, but the green suits me better, although it doesn't fit as well—do you have it in yellow?'

'But I still don't think you'll have much fun, Kore.' Ilone was gently insistent. 'And I think, if you're taking a holiday from work, you should have a rest. Here, where it's quiet and peaceful. Athens is so noisy, even in the winter.'

Kore abandoned any intention of behaving like a good Greek girl. 'I don't want a rest,' she shouted belligerently. 'I want a change. Jo's said I may go and Papa's agreed, so I'm going!'

'And the Apostolakis family, they're going to be very disappointed, especially Serghios. He was only saying how little he'd seen of you this past summer . . .'

'Serghios can go to hell!' Kore muttered almost under her breath, but Joanna caught the words and bit her lip hard to stop herself from grinning.

'Another thing I was thinking about,' she broke the silence which was becoming unbearable, filled as it was with the atmosphere of Kore's stinging temper, Ilone's resentment and Arkady's bland ignoring of both. 'I don't think Ilone's house will be suitable—at least, not as convenient as a hotel.' She had never been inside the place, but Arkady had taken her past it once, pointing it out to her—a small house behind a high wall in a quiet street, a cul-de-sac not far from the Platia Varvana, and she didn't want to stay there. The thought of sleeping in a bed which Arkady might have shared with Ilone sickened her. 'I don't suppose your house boasts a cot, does it?' She kept her voice cool as she posed the question.

Ilone shrugged, a delicate movement of her shoulders, and accompanied it with an understanding smile. 'No, Joanna, but you could always buy one. I'm sure Arkady wouldn't consider it a waste of money.'

'But I should.' Joanna gave back the smile with interest. 'A hotel would provide a cot for free, and since we have a perfectly good one here already, I don't see the point in wasting money. Besides, it's going to cost a fortune in taxi fares to get to the shopping centres. And a hotel would be better in the evenings, there'd be more life for Kore.'

It was a good argument and she hoped—with her fingers crossed—that her husband wouldn't poke holes in it. Her wish was granted. Arkady nibbled at a glutinous mixture of nuts and honey, washed it down with a cup of coffee and nodded approvingly.

'The hotel we used on the way here?' and for Kore's benefit, 'An old-fashioned place with a sprinkling of tourists, and the food and accommodation is first class.'

Athens was as beautiful in the winter as in the summer. Joanna thought it must be the light which seemed to radiate from the old stones of the Acropolis. It was as if they had absorbed all the sunlight during the hot, dry months so that they glowed golden as though they were filled with it. Sheer imagination, of course, as she told herself—this lower end of Greece was enjoying the benefit of being on the end of a ridge of high pressure—and it was certainly dryer than Corfu.

There were a few squally showers blown in by a cold wind, but in between them, the sunlight was dazzling, so it was quite usual to see men in heavy overcoats and sunglasses. The Greeks didn't seem to mind the chilly wind, but a few spots of rain was enough to drive them into the nearest *kafénion*, where they immediately started arguing, laughing or just talking with a great deal of gesticulation over innumerable cups of coffee until the rain stopped.

The business which had brought Arkady to Athens remained a mystery to Joanna. Apparently 'business' was something females weren't expected to interest themselves in—it was part of the male world, a sort of 'for men only' thing, but whatever it was, Arkady was quite successful at it and he came back to the hotel after his short morning consultations, which were always followed by very long 'business' lunches, looking content.

On the second day of their stay, he produced a

collapsible pram, which turned out to be very useful. The hotel was reasonably near the better of the shopping centres, so Joanna and Kore took turns pushing it about the streets while Kore spent some of her carefully hoarded wages and tips. A pair of handmade sandals, made while she waited, some fabulous leather things, shoes made to measure in a shop just off Kolinaki Square, a French-cut suit from one of the boutiques in Niki Street and even a string of worry beads to pin to the hood of Dion's pram. Joanna noticed that never once did her stepdaughter ask, 'Do you think this suits me?' Kore had all her father's self-confidence and her taste, like his, was conservative. Better than that, the tautness, the spats of irritability and temper disappeared and the girl became very easy to get along with.

As for herself, Arkady had said they would start right back at the beginning again, and he had obviously meant it. Dion's cot was set up between their two single beds, and except for an occasional hand beneath Joanna's elbow to help her down steps or pilot her across a street, dodging the crazy traffic, he hardly ever touched her. Illogically, this offended her. It kept her awake at night while she reasoned it out. It was the kind of relationship she had stipulated, yet it wasn't in the least satisfactory.

In the darkness she could hear his quiet, easy breathing, Dion's little snuffle, and with a sigh at her inability to sleep, she reached out to switch on her bedside lamp. In its dim glow she saw Arkady turn on to his back and his eyes were open—like a cat, she thought, asleep one moment and wide awake the next, no in-betweens.

'Can't you sleep?' It was a soft murmur and he turned his head to look at her. In the dimness, it was impossible to tell what sort of face he was wearing, his features were as if she was seeing them through a dark veil. Something fierce cramped her stomach so that she cringed with the pain of it, but she kept her low murmur on a practical level.

'No. If it doesn't bother you, the light, I mean, I think I'll read a bit.' The fierce thing took hold of her again and almost shook her so that she trembled and the hand she reached to the bedside table for a book was visibly unsteady.

He closed his eyes once more and Joanna flicked through the pages of the book, not reading, not even seeing the blocks of print, and she was going too fast—nobody could read at the rate at which she was turning the pages. She tried to concentrate, but the type was a blur, and when he spoke again, softly, she was almost relieved.

'You're not ill?'

'No! There's nothing the matter with me.' She turned another page, seeing nothing for the mist of tears in her eyes. 'I just can't sleep.'

'A drink, perhaps.' She kept her eyes on the printed page and heard the soft rustle as Arkady tossed back the sheet which covered him. The hotel was tourist-orientated and there was a small fridge in the room as well as a machine for making coffee. There was the soft pad of his feet as he walked across the floor. 'Hot or cold?'

'Cold.' Joanna spoke through clenched teeth, afraid they might chatter if she relaxed the pressure of her jaws. With her eyes still on her book, she heard the opening of the fridge door, the tinkle of glasses, the little noise of a bottle being opened and the pad of his feet as he came towards her and just stood there at the side of her bed until she would look up.

Her hands tightened on the book and she stared unseeingly at the pages, feeling the chill of perspiration on her forehead. He knew very well what he was at—he would be standing there, mother-naked—Arkady never wore anything in bed—and it would be more than she could bear. This was another of those times—there had been so many of them while she was alone in London, both before and after Dion had been born, when she had wanted him desperately and when she had flayed herself with her tongue, calling herself all the names she could think of—weak, stupid, insane, lustful—but it hadn't been so bad when she was at one end of a continent and Arkady was at the other.

Now he was in the room and beside her. If she turned her head even slightly, she would see him, his black hair rumpled into curls where he had rubbed it against the pillow, the lamplight gleaming on the smooth skin of his shoulders, glinting on the dark fuzz of hair on his chest which ran arrowlike downwards. She had read of women who had a compulsive desire for one man, but she had never thought she would be one of them— weak and foolish, so that it didn't matter what that man had done, how he had hurt, would go on hurting.

'Drink, Joanna.' His hand slid into the pool of light cast by the lamp—wine, but not in a wineglass, in a plain, rather thick tumbler, and her hands were clenched so tightly on the book, she

couldn't take it from him—her fingers felt as
though they were glued to the cover. Slowly and
with a great deal of effort, she shook her head.

'No,' her mouth was so dry she could hardly
speak except in a hoarse mutter, 'I don't want . . .'

'Then what *do* you want?' He reached across her
and set the glass down on the table calmly and
precisely in the centre of a small mat. 'Then do
you want me, *agape*? I hope so, because I very
much want my wife!'

Tears—they should have been of shame for her
weakness, but they felt more like relief at having
everything made so easy for her—welled up at last
to spill over and run down her face. 'I can't . . .'
she whispered, determined to explain that while
her poor, silly body could ignore Ilone, her mind
couldn't, but the words wouldn't come out. 'I
can't,' she repeated despairingly. 'You don't
understand . . .'

'I understand more than you think.' Arkady
slid down on to the bed beside her, grimacing
ruefully at its narrowness as he drew the book
from her fingers and tossed it on to the floor
where it fell with a soft, dull thud. 'And I know
need when I see it, *agape*. This,' his finger
brushed her mouth, outlining it and lingering on
the soft fullness of her lower lip before he trailed
it down her throat. 'This,' the finger lingered on
a spot where a pulse beat furiously before it
moved on downwards. 'And this,' his hand
closed over her breast.

'I suppose you would,' croaked Joanna, holding
herself rigid while she fought the insidious warmth
that threatened to turn her into a mess of
quivering eagerness. 'Yes, of course you would,'

she added bitterly. 'All that experience—you must have learned something from it.'

'Joanna,' she could feel his tongue caressing her ear and shuddered away from it. 'You knew about that "experience" when you married me. I didn't spell it out in words for you, I didn't think it was necessary. I gave you credit for some intelligence. Kore is sixteen now; my wife died when she was five years old. I had no desire at that time to marry again, so for ten years . . .'

Anger was her only weapon and she summoned up as much as she could muster. '. . . for ten years you were on the loose, and even after that, after you'd married me, you had your little affair. Oh, don't bother to deny it—I've told you, I *saw* you! You and Ilone—and don't you dare to try telling me it was all brotherly because she's some relation to your first wife. I *saw*!'

'And if I told you . . .'

'I don't want to talk about it.' Joanna tried to prise his hand away from her breast where it was damaging her will-power and her morale, failed, and hunched a shoulder ungraciously as she closed her lips firmly.

'You condemn me on one small episode . . .'

'I saw,' she repeated dully, 'and it didn't look so small to me. Like I said, I don't want to talk about it any more,' she added, almost wishing she could confront him with everything because, to be perfectly fair—put the way he had put it, it sounded as if she had made mountains out of molehills. She would have liked to make some nasty remark about breeding stock, but she daren't. Not without implicating Kore.

'Then I was right in my thinking.' Out of the

corner of her eye she caught the quick twitch of his eyebrows, the grown-up counterpart of Dion's little frown. 'You had already begun to regret our marriage,' and as her mouth opened to deny it, he silenced her with a quick shake of his head. 'It didn't happen all at once, I'd noticed the difference in you for quite a little while—and you seized on the first excuse to run away, to put a continent between us.'

'Preferable to asking you for an explanation and being fobbed off with lies and evasions...' The fierce longing in her was now a real physical pain and she ground the words out between her teeth while she held herself motionless by sheer willpower.

'But now you're back,' Arkady pointed out, 'and you're still my wife. If you bite your lip any harder, you'll make it bleed—and you want me.'

'Like hell I do!' Joanna was nearly at the end of her tether and all she could think about was putting some space between them. Alone, away from the touch of his hands, she could cope. It would be bad, but she'd coped before. 'Leave me alone!' she hissed as his hand stroked her hip—it felt very cool against the heat of her skin. 'Oh, you fiend, you bastard!' it came out on a sob. 'Can't you, just for once, play fair?'

'I'm being perfectly fair—by my standards.' Arkady sounded amused as he subdued her futile wriggling without much difficulty. 'It would ease your conscience if I denied everything, told you you'd made a mistake, but why should I make things easy for you? For a year, until you ran away, I treated you with kid gloves, but now you're going to learn to be a good Greek wife and get your priorities right. First in your life comes your husband, then your children, and the rest of your time you devote to your home. If I do anything that displeases you, you may throw things at me—if you do anything to displease me I shall beat you, but there will be no more sulky silences or silly withdrawals. I shall have you when I want you, and I shan't neglect your needs. You'll have everything I can give you and you will find it enough!'

'Very well.' Joanna stopped struggling with him and copied some of his brazenness. 'Make love to me, if that's what you want. I might even enjoy every moment of it—but tomorrow morning, you'll see, nothing will have changed.'

'You were my wife for a year and you believe that?' He sounded disgusted.

'You tried it the first night we arrived on Corfu,' she reminded him, 'and it didn't get us anywhere.'

'Only because, like a fool, I waited for you to make the next move. I thought the love was still there, that the thing between us had survived,' Arkady was murmuring against her throat and she was dizzy with pleasure as his hands stripped away her thin covering, but the spark of rebellion had not quite died.

'I want you,' she admitted baldly. 'I want you, but I don't love you, so it's humiliating. I despise myself—you rob me of my self-respect.'

'Such nonsense!' He reached across her and switched off the lamp before he drew her close, murmuring approval as her arms went about his shoulders, her lips parted beneath his demanding ones and her slender body arched involuntarily against him.

And in the darkness, there was the remembering—how he liked to be touched, the way his muscles tapered away. Arkady was no stranger to hard, physical work, his modest success had been founded on it—His enthusiasm, as if he was doing everything for the first time—that he loved life and everything that went with it. And in everything there was a care and courtesy so that she would have the same pleasure as he found in simple, old-fashioned lovemaking.

'We have been here for two weeks and that is as long as I can spare. We will go home tomorrow.' Arkady made the announcement over the usual breakfast of hot rolls and coffee in the hotel dining room, and Joanna came down to earth with a bump. For the last seven days she had studiously avoided thinking about the future. And they had been good days—Kore had become friendly with the teenage daughter of an English couple who were enjoying a late holiday, going off on expeditions with them, very merry and carefree, to act as their interpreter, introducing them to the joys of *kaféñions* and the ubiquitous kiosks, and, as she said, steering them well away from the Flea Market where everything was either fake or rubbish.

Meanwhile Joanna, despite the fact she had seen it all before, saw it all again, with Arkady carrying Dion at her side. All her favourite places—the Parthenon, looking just as beautiful in the winter sunlight, the Theatre of Dionysus—because of Dion; a trip on the underground to the Turkolimano—the little, almost circular 'Turkish' harbour ringed with small restaurants. Daphni and the fortified monastery, and lastly an afternoon drive out to Cape Sounion to stand in the Temple of Poseidon on top of the towering cliff and watch as the setting sun painted the twelve columns a rosy pink.

And now it had all come to an end—tomorrow she would be back on Corfu and Ilone would be waiting, like a blight, to settle on them and spoil all Joanna's memories. She flicked a quick glance at Kore and discovered a very bleak expression on her stepdaughter's face—as though she didn't want to go home either.

There was a hurried trip to the Plaka where, in the maze of narrow streets, Joanna and Kore shopped for last-minute Christmas presents—a long, lazy dinner with the English couple and their daughter to the accompaniment of an electric bouzouki player murdering the latest pop songs, noisily and cheerfully. Joanna watched as Kore and the English girl exchanged addresses—the English couple were also leaving tomorrow—and grinned as her volatile stepdaughter alternately wept and laughed.

Tomorrow—Joanna fed Dion, changed him and tucked him into the cot, while one part of her wished tomorrow would never come.

CHAPTER SEVEN

ANNA had gone to town on the 'welcome home' dinner and her happiness to see them back was obvious. The lemon-flavoured chicken soup hadn't been burned, the stuffed vine leaves showed no sign of scorching and the sauce she had made to accompany the pilaf of shrimps and prawns was quite smooth. Her one failure was an orange soufflé, and that only looked sad because it had sunk in the middle—it tasted all right.

Ilone, as usual, was looking beautiful, with the kind of polished perfection which could only come from long hours of preparation. Joanna wished she could have the same sort of dedication, get everything just right, but she hadn't the patience or the time—when she had finished feeding Dion, there was barely a quarter of an hour in which she had to shower and change. Her glance went on past Ilone to Kore, who seemed to have lost some of the effervescent sparkle she had shown in Athens.

But that was to be expected, Joanna comforted herself. Kore was missing her English friend—a very nice girl—and all she had was a prettily coloured silk scarf and an address on a page torn from a diary. Here, there was nobody she could talk to on her own level, nobody with whom to discuss the relative merits of pop groups or hash over Clint Eastwood's performance in his latest film. Kore would be better tomorrow when she was back at work and had some company of her own age.

Arkady was being urbanely smooth, sharing himself between his womenfolk—a soothing remark in Greek for Ilone—why in hell's name did she need soothing?—a little joke with his daughter, something about a visit she wanted to make to England to see her new friend and which he said wasn't possible at the moment. Whereat it ceased to be a joke to Kore and her scowl was nearly as magnificent as her father's.

Anna brought in the hard *feta* cheese and the pot of Greek coffee, and Joanna, with a muttered excuse, fled. She didn't care for the cheese and she had never been able to manage the coffee, always she ended up with a mouthful of grounds and sediment—besides, it was very strong and kept her awake. Arkady produced a bottle of Greek brandy, and she didn't care for that either. Some people raved about it, but as far as she was concerned, it was like drinking liquid gelignite. It slid down her throat and exploded as it hit her stomach.

Upstairs in the bedroom, she occupied some time unpacking and sorting through her things, pattering between cases and drawers, cases and wardrobe and cases and laundry basket, until everything was disposed of and the empty luggage could be strapped up and put away. Dion cooed from his crib—he was getting a bit big for it, the wickerwork creaked ominously with his smallest movement; it would soon be time to bring out the cot for him—and she picked him up and seated herself in a low chair with him on her lap.

He was demanding but not fretfully so, his

snuffles had stopped and his chest sounded less ominous, but the travelling and the alteration in his routine hadn't pleased him.

'A bit too much of being carried about and made a fuss of,' Joanna told him as she poked him gently in the tummy. He rewarded her with a wide smile and a noise which sounded like 'hello' but was a pure accident as she went on. 'Attention, that's what you want—just like the rest of the male sex!'

'And what has the male sex done to offend you, *agape*?' Arkady hadn't lingered downstairs, he had come in silently and was standing behind her, peering at his son over her shoulder.

'They're demanding,' she tossed the words over her shoulder at him without turning her head. 'Look at this one, he's not yet five months old, but already he's showing all the signs of being the complete male chauvinist. Spoiled rotten, that's what he is!'

'And who does most of the spoiling?' Arkady bent over her, one hand on her shoulder while with the other he spanned his son's small chest. 'His doting mother, of course. Shouldn't he start being weaned soon?'

'Trying to get rid of me already?' Joanna put as much humour into the question as possible. These last few days had been wonderful, but once bitten, twice shy—she still couldn't allow herself to be sure of her position—she didn't dare! It was a tricky business, living each day as if it might be her last. True, Arkady seemed to have some sort of future planned out for them, but that planning had taken place while he was outside Ilone's orbit, well away from her sphere of influence. Who could tell if, now he was back, he wouldn't regret, start changing his mind? His answer when it came was comforting, depending which way you looked at it.

'Only so that you may have a little more time to yourself, my dear,' and, almost as an afterthought, 'And more time for me, of course.'

'Elegantly put.' Joanna gulped on disappointment—why couldn't he have said something concrete and romantic like "I'll never let you go"? Something she could rely on. 'And with just the right amount of altruism to stop you sounding dead selfish!'

He laughed at her waspish tone. 'All men are selfish, you said so yourself, *agape*, so concentrate on your other male chauvinist while I get a shower.'

'As my master commands.' She dipped her head in mock deference. 'And don't steal all the hot water!' she called at his retreating back.

Arkady was gone in the morning when Joanna woke. Where, she didn't know, but probably on some 'business' which he didn't expect her to understand so hadn't bothered to tell her about. Would she ever get used to a husband who wrapped his life up into two separate compartments marked 'HIS' and 'HERS'?

But already little Sylvie was bustling quietly about, opening curtains to let in light, opening windows to let in the cool, damp air and softly singing something very Greek and sad, reminiscent of the *syrtaki* music—later Joanna recognised it as coming from *Zorba the Greek*, but for now it seemed just to be in keeping with the mist-laden air and the dark green of cypress, which always reminded Joanna of funerals and graveyards.

'*Kalimera*, Kyria Joanna.' Sylvie was already bringing across a tray of tea and perforce Joanna had to struggle into a sitting position to receive it on her knees. This child was waiting on her and she should be ashamed of herself to allow it! Yet Sylvie seemed to be enjoying it. Joanna made a wry face and poured a cup of tea—the girl was probably glad she and Dion were back, that she was on her own, crackling starchily round the bedroom instead of being completely under her dragon of a grandmother's eagle eye. Anna ought to have some help in the kitchen, but it would have to be arranged most diplomatically or she would burn everything in sight.

She watched as Sylvie lifted Dion out of the crib, her thin little arms hardly looking strong enough for the task, but there was no hesitation about her—that was what practice did for you. Joanna smiled ruefully as she recalled her own first amateurish fumblings.

'He doesn't want feeding yet, not until nearly eleven o'clock,' she said slowly; Sylvie's English was good but not that good.

'I play with him a little,' Sylvie explained seriously. 'Is good for him.'

So Joanna swung herself out of bed and hurried off to the bathroom leaving the two children playing together. As she dressed, she indulged in a little mythological meandering. What had fate in store for her today?—but there were three fates. Calm, detached Clotho who held the distaff; busy Lachesis, spinning the thread, and severe and impersonal Atropos with her shears ready to cut the thread. Which one was waiting for her? Ilone, in the guise of Atropos, she judged—shears sharpened and waiting to sever the slender strand that bound Joanna and Arkady together—it *must* be Atropos!

But when Joanna arrived in the dining-room for a rather late breakfast, she found it deserted, so after a hurried cup of coffee, a roll and honey and another coffee, she made her way to the kitchen and forcibly helped Anna until it was time to feed Dion. After she had attended to her son, she returned to the kitchen, this time with bits of cotton wool poked in her ears so she didn't hear Anna's crossness. Anna was an old woman who needed help, so she was going to have help whether she liked it or not!

The day passed without a sight of Ilone except at lunchtime, when she emerged from her room, smelling strongly of lavender scented eau de cologne and complaining of a headache—she returned to it after swallowing precisely two spoonsful of chicken soup and apparently spent the time between lunch and dinner in martyred isolation. Atropos had not sharpened her shears sufficiently. She had tried them out by complaining about the noise of the vacuum cleaner, but her complaints fell on deaf ears—Joanna's because she still had the cotton wool in place and Anna's because the cook had taken umbrage over the wasted soup and wasn't in the mood to hear anything.

At half past six, Arkady and his daughter returned together in the Range Rover, surprising Joanna by saying they had been together all day.

'Not at the hotel?' Joanna raised an enquiring eyebrow at her stepdaughter.

'I don't have to if I don't want to.' Kore lapsed

into near surliness. 'I could go there if I wanted to, but it's so boring now that all the summer visitors have gone—there just isn't enough to keep me occupied. Besides, Papa offered to take me to Paxos where there was some real work for me. The two new villas, Jo—you should see them now that the bathroom furniture Papa ordered while we were in Athens has been installed. Papa says he'll be taking you over soon to take the photographs of the interiors—for the brochures, you know. I wish the villas in Crete were finished.' A momentary enthusiasm lit her eyes but soon went out, leaving them large, dark and somehow haunted.

Kore had something on her mind—Joanna thought it might be the Apostolakis thing, and if it was, she didn't blame Kore. A future built around young Serghios wasn't her idea of a maiden's dream of love everlasting. If it had anything to do with her—but it hadn't!—Kore wasn't her daughter, and even had she been, Joanna wouldn't have been consulted. Damn this male-orientated Greek way of thinking, of living where men went off to their 'business' and made all the decisions, even entertained the visitors while the women walked about silently with saucepans in their hands!

By the time Arkady and Kore had washed and changed and Ilone had conquered her headache sufficiently to feel well enough to join them it was nearly eight o'clock—then there was a lot of talk while Ilone and Arkady fortified themselves with glasses of ouzo while Kore and Joanna settled for ginger beer, so it was nearly nine before Anna started serving dinner, and Joanna groaned. The meal could take anything up to a couple of hours, which meant that as usual she would miss the dessert course.

At just gone ten Joanna, bearing a small bunch of seedless grapes, left the table and went up to attend Dion, who was wide awake, kicking and uttering bad-tempered squawks. He glared at her angrily and she stifled his further cries by lifting him out of the crib, whereat his small face put on a beaming smile. She had only just begun to feed him when there was a tap at the door and Kore came in.

'Papa's talking about this school again.' She plumped herself down on the edge of the bed and scowled. 'What would it be like, Jo?'

'I haven't the faintest idea.'

'You mean you didn't go to one of them?' Kore registered surprise.

'No,' Joanne shook her head serenely. 'My parents were both dead, I lived with an elderly aunt and there wasn't sufficient money for me to be sent to a place like that. It was more important that I learned to earn my own living.'

'Ilone says I'll be taught lots of things—how to run a house, how to dress, give dinner parties and things like that. She says it will give me self-confidence. But I don't see why I should go if I don't want to—you didn't, and you get along all right. I wouldn't mind if I could go now, but I'd have to wait till next year, Papa says. They're down there, Papa and Ilone,' Kore's dark head jerked to indicate the lounge-cum-dining-room, 'talking about it.' Her mouth curved in a derisory smile. 'They needn't bother, I'm not going. Sometimes I think they're just trying to get rid of me!'

'I'm sure your father has your best interests at heart,' Joanna said stiltedly—for some reason, she didn't like the idea that Arkady consulted Ilone about Kore's future. She tried to be broadminded about it, telling herself that after all, Ilone was some sort of relation to Kore, that she was bound to be concerned about the girl, but being nicely broadminded didn't help when she was seething with jealousy. Imagining all sorts of things— fiercely jealous of the influence Ilone had over Arkady, the way he listened to her—really listened. She thought of them together in the dimly lighted room, talking softly while their eyes said so much more than the words that passed between them—She stood up suddenly, jolting Dion so that he gave a yell of startled surprise. Swiftly she hushed him, watched his eyelids droop and laid him back in the crib, noting idly that her hands weren't quite as steady as she would have liked them to be.

'But why don't you leave it for a while?' Joanna found her voice and kept it cool and steady. 'There's no point in worrying about something which might never happen—next year's a long time away and I'm sure nobody's trying to get rid of you. Your papa loves you very much . . .'

'But next year,' Kore refused to be comforted, 'I'll be nearly eighteen and they'll start on this "let's get married" thing, and I don't want to be married for years and years, especially if they're still thinking about spotty, fat Serghios. Oh, Jo, I thought you'd be different, but you're not. Wait and see, that's what you all tell me, and I don't want to wait, I want it all arranged *now*!' And with a disgusted snort, she stamped out.

'And you're not the only one!' Joanna said silently to the panels of the closed door. 'Only you're young, you'll grow out of it.' Wearily, she undressed and huddled herself into bed. She'd been a fool to think that being a proper wife to Arkady would make any difference. It had worked well enough in Athens, like a second honeymoon, but once back here, it seemed to make very little difference—pillow talk was all they had, and even then he never mentioned love—only wanting and need. 'Your trouble is you're a jealous bitch,' she told herself. 'Jealous and suspicious, utterly lacking in self-confidence—if anybody needs a year at a posh finishing school, it's you!'

'You're not asleep, *agape*, so stop pretending you are.' Arkady ruthlessly straightened her out from her curled-up remoteness and turned her towards him. 'Anna tells me you've been helping in the kitchen. It's not necessary. If she needs help—and I suppose she does, she's nearly seventy—we'll find a woman to come in daily.'

'And have civil war?' Joanna seethed at his stupidity. 'She'd harry the life out of the woman, never let her do a thing except scrub the floor, because she'd be afraid you'd not want her any more. I'm about the only person she'd tolerate because she can't stop me. Besides, I like to be busy. I'm not used to sitting around and being waited on. If I was in London, I'd be seeing about getting myself a job, maybe even have opened a photographic studio.'

'You feel fit enough for it?' With a finger beneath her chin, he tipped her face up so that the lamplight shone on it. 'Yes, you look much better, so if you want work—your own type of work—

I've some for you to do. The villas on Patras, I'd like to get the interior pictures ready next week so that the brochures can be issued to the travel agents early in January.'

'That's cutting it a bit fine. Most of the others will be on the shelves already and bookings will have started . . .'

'Mmm,' he pulled her close and rested his cheek on her hair. 'But we'll just have to take a chance. Will it be too uncomfortable for Dion to travel in my boat? We could always take the ferry.'

'Your boat, I think.' Joanna was getting sleepy and the words came out on a yawn. 'That's if you can guarantee to do the trip in less time than the ferry takes. Now, that *is* an uncomfortable vessel, just the one little saloon, although I don't suppose it will be so crowded now that the season's over.' And with another enormous yawn, she drifted off to sleep.

When she woke in the morning—Dion slept all night now and rarely disturbed her before eight o'clock—Arkady and Kore were gone. Off to Paxos, so Sylvie prattled on, where the Thespinis Kore was to decide on tiles for the villa bathrooms and also the colours for the bedrooms.

'I hope she chooses yellow or beige.' Joanna was a bit disgruntled at missing the fun, but she cheered up when she thought of the things she would have to do—clean and check her cameras, buy film and batteries for her flash-guns, see what she could get in the way of auxiliary lighting—it was a pity she'd let her own stuff go, but there'd been nowhere to keep it . . .

'So none of your nonsense this morning,' she told her son severely. 'Your mum's going to be busy. She hasn't time to play games today.'

Half an hour later, she bounced off along the mule track to Krini in the beach buggy on her way to Paleokastritsa, leaving Dion in Sylvie's charge, Ilone still immured in her room and Anna swelling with visible relief at having her kitchen to herself.

'The *kyria* should go out more,' she had said, her withered face cracking into a smile as she skilfully boned chickens. 'It is why Kyrios Arkady brought Sylvie to the house,' she continued flatly. 'It is better so! The *kyria* has others to consider, she should not give all her time, all her love to her child—it should be shared.'

And that's telling you! Joanna grinned to herself at the mild stricture—mild by Anna's standards but oh, so correct. She remembered the long hours she had spent in her darkroom, working on black and white negatives—portraits mostly—there wasn't so much fun, you couldn't do so much with a colour film. She had given it all up when she had married Arkady, and she had been wrong to do so.

Joanna was so busy planning portraits of Dion, of Sylvie—that should be a worthwhile subject, the child was beautiful and utterly unselfconscious—of Kore in all her moods—Arkady, a low key effect with perhaps only two lamps, one for background and a soft modelling one off to one side so that his bone structure would show.

Paleokastritsa hadn't much to offer except film—moderately fresh and both black and white and colour, but not a single photoflood bulb to be had, which was disappointing. If she couldn't get the bulbs in time, there was another way round it; she could fix the flashgun to the tripod and bounce the flash off the ceiling. It wasn't the best way to do it, but it would serve, if the ceilings weren't too high. Slightly disappointed, she wandered into a taverna with her large bag of assorted film and ordered herself a coffee, continental, not Greek.

Halfway through her second cup, a voice from behind her made her turn her head. 'Well, hello, ma'am! May I sit at your table?'

Hank Sommers walked round and pulled out a chair for himself with all the aplomb of a personable young man who was used to being welcome anywhere, and Joanna, who had been deep in the construction of a portrait of Sylvie and Dion—the patio with the curve of arched plasterwork above their heads, side lit, and the negatives treated to give a grainy effect—smiled at him absently.

'Long time, no see,' he continued, drawling out the words. 'Kore's taken to hiding herself.'

'She's been in Athens for a while.' Joanna made it a gentle explanation. 'We all have, and Kore was in need of a holiday.' And as a girl came running with a bottle of ouzo, a glass and a jug of water, 'You know this place?'

'I lodge here, ma'am. A couple of rooms,' he indicated upstairs with a wave of his hand. 'Nice and peaceful—in the winter.' His smile to the waitress was just right—wide, uncomplicated and grateful—it rocked the girl back on her heels before he turned his attention back to Joanna, eyeing her large plastic bag. 'You been doing some marketing, ma'am?'

'Film for my cameras.' She peeped into the bag. 'I was really surprised, even the black and white stuff's quite fresh, and that I didn't expect—most tourists use colour, either print or reversal, nowadays. I thought I'd have to hunt high and low for the other.'

'You can thank me for that, ma'am,' he smiled at her, and looked almost shy. 'I've been doing a bit of serious work—well, it seemed a shame using my little old Rolliecon for colour snaps all the time. I've been doing some close-ups; old fishermen, pretty young girls, you know the sort of thing. If they're any good, maybe I'll have me an exhibition when I get home. But you look kind of disappointed, ma'am. Was there anything you couldn't get?'

'Mmm,' she stirred her coffee. 'I wanted some photofloods, but,' she shrugged, 'I'll have to try Corfu town, they don't have any here, or have them flown in from Athens.'

'Maybe I can help you after all,' Hank smiled at her, and almost against her will, Joanna became aware of his charm even through the little flicker of something like distrust that filled her. He certainly had charisma of a sort, she could hardly blame Kore for finding him attractive. It wasn't a charisma like Arkady's—that went so deep, right through to his backbone, and then started coming out the other side—she smiled at herself for such a ludicrous thought. No, Hank Sommers' charm was a light, surface thing and she thought it didn't go very deep. Like one of those showy flowers that wilted if it was dry or cold because the roots weren't deep and strong enough to support it in anything but ideal conditions—Cultivated, that was what it was.

'Yes, ma'am, I guess I can help you after all,' Hank's slightly nasal voice cut through her musings. 'I've got a couple of floods, the five-hundred-watt ones, with reflectors and on light-weight stands. I haven't used them much, so you should get a few hours out of them before they burn out, and you're truly welcome to them, ma'am, and you can bring them back any old time. You stay there, while I go and collect them,' and he was off, through the door that led to the private parts of the house, and she heard his footsteps on the stairs.

Joanna had to force herself to wait. She didn't want to—she didn't want to be beholden. She could also be putting her foot in it, especially as Kore had given the impression of having gone off Hank, and what was worse, she had become aware of several curious glances from other patrons of the taverna. Fool that she was, she should have remembered she was now in Greece and that married women didn't meet casual male acquaintances, much less sit talking to them in public places. She could only hope she'd been taken for yet another tourist!

'You'll remember me to Kore, ma'am?' Hank had come back with the floods, all neatly packed in a large flat case, and Joanna did her best to be cool about thanking him for the loan and getting out of the taverna as quickly as possible. She should never have gone there in the first place, but she just hadn't been thinking—she would have had equally good coffee at one of the hotels, something which was considered quite respectable!

Knowing it was useless trying to keep a secret in this small place, she poured out the tale of her day's activities over dinner that evening, rather surprised at the reactions from Arkady and his daughter. Ilone's was predictable, as was her expression of frozen distaste, but Joanna didn't care about that. Whatever she had done, had been done openly and innocently—and an enormous frown knitted her eyebrows—not like some she could mention *and* touch with a very short stick!

Arkady merely smiled and there was no censure in it; he even teased her a bit, his deep voice drowning out Ilone's muttered expostulations, but Joanna very nearly ignored him as she turned to Ilone.

'You were saying?' She raised an eyebrow and the jut of her small chin was belligerent. 'I thought I heard you mention something about unacceptable behaviour, but if my husband accepts it, surely that's good enough. His——' she turned an innocently sweet smile on the husband, 'his is the only opinion I care about. By modern standards, I think I behaved beautifully. I didn't even offer him a cup of my coffee.'

But it was Kore's reaction that had surprised her, almost taken her breath away. The girl had gone quite rigid and her expression made Joanna think of somebody who had found the ground cracking right under their feet. Just for a second, her stepdaughter had looked frightened to death, but when she looked again, Kore was back to normal and only the whitening of her knuckles on the hand holding her fork indicated any stress, but she dismissed it for the present. It would all come out in the open at some time; Kore was very bad at keeping secrets.

'So,' Joanna continued smoothly as she finished what remained on her plate—Anna's dish of boiled meat balls on a bed of rice tasted wonderful—'I'm all ready to go. My cameras are clean and loaded and I've got the photofloods I need. Which reminds me, Arkady,' she looked at her husband with a wide smile, 'I'll have to have replacements for those bulbs, so could you . . .?'

'Mmm,' he nodded. 'We'll go tomorrow, and on the way back we'll call in at Kerkira. If we can't get what you want there, there may be a little delay. Will that matter very much?'

'Shouldn't think so.' She laid down her fork and wiped her mouth with a napkin. 'So, if you'll excuse me . . .' and with another bright smile, she left the table and hurried to the bedroom where Dion was making his presence heard, loudly and hungrily.

Not many minutes later Kore tapped at the door and came in to fling herself down on the bedside rug, fingers laced behind her head and her eyes slitted against the lamplight.

'Hank?' she made it an innocent question. 'How's he looking?'

'All of a month older than when I saw him last.' Joanna had Dion on his changing mat and she thought she was getting quite expert at his toilet. 'He said he hadn't seen much of you recently and I told him we'd been in Athens for a holiday—he knew that already, of course.'

'I suppose you've invited him for dinner.' It was a half question and Kore posed it delicately.

'Certainly not.' Joanna kept her head bent over the baby. 'I wouldn't do that, not without asking you first. As a matter of fact, I thought you'd gone off him.' She could see Kore's relief in the relaxation of her body, even feel the whole atmosphere of the room growing less tense.

'I have.' Her stepdaughter rolled over bonelessly and grinned up at her. 'I used to think he was wonderful, full of male sex appeal and charisma, but now I don't. I suppose it's because I hadn't any real men to compare him with. Anybody would look good enough to eat compared with Serghios, wouldn't they?'

'I should think so.' Joanna went on playing with Dion, tickling his tummy until he crowed with delight. 'But why compare him with Serghios?'

'Who else do I have to compare him with?' Kore sounded disgruntled. 'There isn't anybody, Jo, and you know it. The summer visitors, the tourists, they don't count; you can't get to know them properly in the short time they're here, and as for the other Greek boys, like Serghios, they all do what their mamas and papas tell them—it's money, money and money again. There's not a spark of romance in them!'

'Poor you!' Joanna made herself sound unfeeling and then softened it with an understanding smile. 'But it's your own fault in taking Serghios as a standard when you've got a much better one right under your nose. Yes,' at Kore's puzzled look, 'right here. I mean your father, silly, so why don't you stop wondering if the young men you meet are better than Serghios and start asking yourself if they could ever match up to your father? And I can tell you, Hank Sommers doesn't, not in any way. What put you off Hank anyway—did somebody say he was too old for you?'

'He isn't as nice as I thought he was,' Kore scrambled to her knees, 'and I don't love him or anything like that. He was just a friend, you know. Somebody to have a Coke with, to talk to—and,' she became devastatingly honest, 'I only did it because everybody said I shouldn't.'

'Which is the worst of all possible reasons and

liable to get you into more trouble than you bargain for.' Joanna kept her reprimand soft and gentle. 'Now, having got that lot off your chest, off to bed with you, we've got a busy day tomorrow.'

'Oh Jo, I *do* love you,' Kore giggled. 'You say the funniest things! Get that lot off my chest—I've never heard that before!'

CHAPTER EIGHT

THE boat trip to Paxos wasn't very comfortable. A strong westerly wind was gusting, bringing squally showers of cold rain and whipping the sea into choppy waves. Kore was enjoying every pitch and toss of the little cabin cruiser, Dion slept through it all, Arkady stood at the wheel, quite unperturbed, but Joanna enviously eyed a large and stately yacht which was beating its way south under full sail. The graceful curve of the knife-edge prow cut through the waves, whereas the small cabin cruiser bucketed up and down from peak to trough in a very sickmaking way.

Fortunately, before she felt ill enough to be really sick, the brief storm had passed over; the wind had died, the clouds cleared and the sun was shining out of a cool blue sky.

'It's often this way,' Arkady comforted her. 'The Mediterranean has to be treated with respect even nowadays. In the old days, before engines, small ships hugged the coastlines for fear of these sudden storms which could blow them off course—toss them about until they didn't know where they were.'

Joanna put a hand on her stomach, which was still queasy. 'Don't talk to me about being tossed about! I'm a very fair weather sailor and I know these storms were the reason Ulysses gave for taking ten years to get from Troy to Ithaca—poor Penelope must have been mad to believe him! He may have had a silver tongue, but it was as crooked as a corkscrew, and if I'd been in her place, I'd have told him to go and get lost again! How much longer before we land?'

'Less than an hour.' Arkady pointed to the chart. 'We'll be going into this bay on the north, Lakkas Bay. That's where the villas are, and there's no shortage of tavernas where we can get a meal before we start work. Did the rough weather upset Dion?'

Joanna couldn't resist a chuckle. 'Not a bit, he slept through it all. My son has the makings of a master mariner.'

'*Our* son,' Arkady reproved her gently.

As they entered Lakkas Bay, the engine of the cabin cruiser throttled down so that they almost drifted in, a round head emerged from the water, two large mournful eyes regarded them gravely, and with hardly a ripple, the seal submerged and swam away before Joanna could even get a camera from its case.

'Damn!' The word came out explosively from her lips and then, mournfully, 'It isn't as if I didn't know there'd be seals . . .'

'Just that you'd forgotten them.' Arkady was equally mournful, although his eyes were laughing at her. 'How short is a woman's memory that she'd forget the seals—and in only a year!' He shook his head.

'A traumatic year,' Joanna defended herself stoutly. 'I had other things on my mind, if you remember.' There was a little thud as the boat nudged against the landing stage, a patter of bare feet as a skinny, agile child came running to catch the mooring rope—laughing over his shoulder at the comrades he had outdistanced—and then the boat was wallowing and Joanna reached out a hand to her husband to steady herself.

'Will you bring the cameras?' She nodded at the boy. 'That's another thing I'd forgotten—how very beautiful and unselfconscious the children are. I'll carry Dion,' she added hastily.

'So,' teased Arkady, 'you'll trust me with your cameras, which wouldn't survive a fall into the water, but not with my son, who would!'

'Papa, Jo, come along!' Kore was already on the rather rickety staging, and Joanna, glad to be interrupted, stepped carefully on to the creaking boards and held out her arms to take her baby.

Paxos looked lushly green with an almost tropical appearance, even this late in the year, and the sunlight, just as brilliant as in summer but lacking the heat, gleamed on Arkady's two new villas perched on the western bluff which overlooked the bay. New plaster shone whitely in contrast to the red-tiled roofs and fresh green paint, making Joanna nod with satisfaction. The brightness was what she wanted, the lack of heat didn't matter, although it wasn't exactly cold. She judged the temperature to be in the sixties—just right for working.

Kore looked longingly at a taverna, but both Joanna and Arkady were firm. 'Work first,' Joanna told her, 'while the light holds. If we wait, it might cloud over, and I'd like to get all the photographs taken today. They'll have to be processed, you see, which means another week before we can send them off. I know,' as an idea struck her, 'why don't you pop into the taverna and get a couple of cans of lemonade, then you can sit on the patio and add a little human interest to the picture.' She raised an eyebrow at her husband. 'It's a well-known fact that a good-looking girl can rake in the customers more easily than a view of bricks and mortar. Would you mind? I mean, I'll take some with and some without Kore, you can make up your own mind . . .'

'Hush!' Arkady's face was alight with laughter as he watched his daughter speeding into the darkness of the taverna. 'Don't make too much of it, *karthia mou*, or Kore will be charging the company a modelling fee!'

The small endearment caught at Joanna's heart, twisting it into a bitter uncertainty which she couldn't explain properly or satisfactorily even to herself. Since the Athens trip, theirs had been a normal marriage, but it lacked something, and as she thought about it, that lack settled in the pit of her stomach, cold, heavy and sending chilly tendrils through her every nerve. As far as the physical side was concerned, Arkady was the perfect husband, but boiled down to the essence, there was still something missing. There was a part of his life she didn't share, a part of his mind which he never let her see. Bodily satisfaction was a wonderful thing, but he never said he loved her. She thought back, right to the beginning, and realised that he never had!

'Something troubles you, Joanna?' Already they were through the small village of Lakka and had turned off on to a mule track that led up to the villas.

'Mmm,' she prevaricated. 'I'm trying to work out which is the heavier, Dion or the camera cases; this infant's beginning to feel like a ton weight and my arm's going dead. Where's Kore? I thought she'd have caught us up by now.'

'Probably gossiping with the people in the taverna,' shrugged Arkady as he dropped the cases and relieved her of the baby, who slept on undisturbed while he picked up the big case containing the floods and their stands, leaving Joanna only with the cameras to carry, and walked on up the track, as surefooted as one of the mules that had made it originally.

With Dion asleep on a bed in one of the north-facing bedrooms where it was cool and dim, Joanna got on with her work. The two villas were identical, so she needed only exterior shots of one, and she couldn't fault the buildings. They were attractive, well built, and nothing had been skimped—they gave an appearance, both outside and in, of restrained luxury. The furniture was the product of a local carpenter, no plastics, only solid wood which would stand a lot of wear and tear. But the path up to the villas! She frowned at the narrow winding of it.

'I hope you're going to do something about that,' she nodded towards it. 'The visitors will be arriving at Gaios, I suppose, and coming on from there by taxi—they're going to blench when they see that track. They'll want to be delivered straight to the door, not have to hump luggage up the hill.'

'It will be improved before the first tenants arr ...' He halted in the middle of the word as Kore made a grand entrance on to the patio. And Kore hadn't been wasting time either. She was wearing a white bikini, Italian, if its brevity was any guide, and her hair, normally constrained in a ponytail, was loose about her shoulders.

'Cover yourself!' Arkady's voice was harsh with disapproval and when his daughter made a sulky face, he went on hardily, 'When you're married, you may wear whatever your husband permits, but while you're in my care, you'll be dressed decently . . .'

'Oh!' Kore tossed her head. 'If you're thinking about Serghios, he'll let me wear whatever I like. As long as he gets the money . . .'

'Which is one reason I've decided against the Apostolakis connection,' Arkady scowled. 'You need somebody to keep you in order, Kore, and Serghios isn't man enough to do it . . .'

The rest of what he was saying was muffled as his daughter flung herself upon him, squealing with happiness. 'Papa, you've made me the happiest girl in the world! I don't want to get married for ages, so don't be in a hurry to find somebody else, and I wasn't going to be photographed like this—*of course!* I'd stick to the plastic cushions on the lounger, wouldn't I? You just wait and see—and it's all my own idea.'

Kore darted back round the house and emerged again seconds later, the bikini covered with a white beach towel draped sarongwise about her youthful body. There was a scarlet hibiscus blossom tucked behind her ear, although whether it was real or plastic, Joanna wouldn't have cared to say.

'And for my next trick!' giggled Kore as she produced a tall, stemmed glass from behind her back. 'I thought a can of lemonade would look cheap and spoil the effect, so I borrowed this from the taverna with a couple of jazzy straws and a cupful of ice-cubes.' She was taking it all very seriously as she lowered herself on to a lounger and took up a languid pose. 'Does that look all right, Jo, or should we put a sprig of something in the top of the glass? I'll hunt for a bit of mint if you like.'

They arrived back at the villa on Corfu in plenty of time to bathe and change for dinner—after stopping off in Corfu town to hand in the rolls of colour print film for processing—and were met at the bottom of the staircase by Ilone, who was in a reproachful mood. The reproach didn't extend as far as Joanna, but that didn't worry her—by this time she had given up all hope that Ilone would ever recognise her presence, greet her or even speak to her. She was included vaguely in the Greek woman's welcoming smile, since it was impossible not to be, but apart from that, she might just as well not have existed.

However, she was very satisfied with her day's work. She had used nearly all the colour film she had bought, and surely, among that many exposures there ought to be half a dozen at least which were good enough for the brochure. And it had been a good day. There had been laughter and companionship—the way she and Kore had fought with a mint green and white striped bedspread to get the stripes exactly right as they had spread it over an unmade bed and how the thing had fought back with a mind of its own so that they had had to arrange it over and over again before Joanna was satisfied.

Lunch at the taverna—how they had left Arkady with a glass of ouzo in front of him and Dion asleep on his knees while she and Kore had gone into the kitchen to choose what they should eat—a purely private meal made especially for them since it was winter and there were no other customers—the creamy taramosalata, the hot fresh rolls a small child had been sent to get—the souvlaki. They had watched the chunks of lamb being grilled and the pride of the proprietor as he had produced a bottle of Demestica because Joanna couldn't drink resinated wine. And finally, the way a young girl, younger even than Sylvie, had calmly removed Dion from Joanna's arms and sat with him on a stool so that his mother could eat her meal undisturbed.

Beneath the shower, Joanna washed her hair free of the salt which had dried in it from the spray flung up when the boat had charged through the choppy seas, and removed the last traces of sand from her body. Life wasn't so bad after all; very few people suffered from a surfeit of unalloyed happiness, or even a modest amount of it. Happiness just depended on lowering one's standards, accepting the good with the bad. It was all very philosophical—she had to count her blessings and, suitably soothed, she emerged from the shower, wrapped herself in an oversized bath sheet and made her way back to the bedroom, to find Arkady looking down at his son, and she knew it was her turn to be generous.

'Thank you for clearing up the Apostolakis business,' she said, and then, with a rueful smile, 'It'll be one less thing for Kore to nag about!'

Arkady raised his head from his contemplation of the baby. 'She has complained?'

'Mmm,' she waved a hand at the empty bathroom. 'You can go in now, I've finished. Will there be any waves?' she asked after a moment, but the noise of the shower drowned out her voice and there was no answer, so she struggled into fresh underwear and pulled a pine green caftan over her head while she waited.

'Will there be any waves?' she repeated the question as Arkady stalked out of the bathroom, a towel wrapped around his lean hips, and started to flick through the hangers in the wardrobe. He tossed a fresh white shirt on to the bed, followed it with a pair of dark, thin pants and an equally thin cardigan. Joanna kept her eyes turned away from him, concentrating on brushing out her hair, but when there was no answer, she was forced to look up to find him looking at her sardonically.

'Not so many as might have been if you hadn't presented me with a son,' he told her almost wickedly. 'Kore's marriage portion decreases proportionately with the number of sons we have. I doubt if the Apostolakis family will make a fuss, they've got plenty of time to make other arrangements for Serghios—Kore is still too young for marriage, but Ilone won't be pleased.'

'Does that matter?' Joanna went on brushing her hair—the dreadful tow colour was nearly gone and it was shining rosy gold where it sprang from her high forehead.

'A little, but not much.' In the mirror she saw him shrug. She also saw that he had both trunks and shirt on, and he was doing up the buttons of the latter, so it was quite safe for her to turn round. Lord, would she ever be able to look at his body without that dread fierceness cramping her stomach? 'Ilone is a relative, about the only one Kore has on her mother's side, and until I remarried, she had almost complete charge of Kore. Perhaps I should have paid more attention to the child, but ...'

'She was only a girl,' Joanna said bitterly. 'But even a daughter needs a father as well as a mother.'

'You tell me that!' Arkady came to stand behind her, his hands on her shoulders. 'When you yourself wanted to deprive Dion of a father? You wanted to bring him up yourself, shut me out completely . . .'

'But would you have blackmailed me, threatened me into sharing him, if he'd been another girl?' she demanded fiercely.

'Yes, I think I would.' He lowered his head so that their two reflections in the mirror were side by side and she watched his mouth curve into an irresistible smile. 'I like to think I've learned from my mistakes. Besides, what would people have thought of me? This is a small island, and Greeks are no different from the rest of humanity when it comes to gossip. I'd have become known as a man who couldn't control his wife.'

'Big deal!' she snorted. 'So I was brought back here to save your precious self-esteem, your public image!'

'No, *agape*.' He stood up, dropping a light kiss on the top of her head en route. 'I brought Dion back because he's mine and his place is with me—and you. I brought you because you're my wife, and also because you're a passionate woman, and like Dion, your place is with me.'

'You twisted my arm!' Joanna's eyes were the grey of polished steel as she glared at him, but he only laughed as he pulled her against him.

'Only a little,' he murmured, 'only a very, very little, and it didn't hurt all that much, did it? Shall we go down to dinner?' And his amusement seemed to increase as she pushed against his chest to free herself and stamped out of the room.

Dinner was not an unqualified success. Anna's food was delicious, Joanna even sampled the *kalamarakia*—she had only tried it once before, in a taverna, and it had been like chewing bits of rubber, but Anna's way with fried pieces of squid made them crisp and quite delicious—but Ilone cast a blight over everything. Joanna grinned to herself—anybody might be forgiven for thinking that Ilone was the one whose marriage plans had gone into the melting pot!

On the other hand, Kore was on top of the world, chattering and laughing, so Joanna sat, feeling alternately chilled and warmed by the draughts of displeasure from one side and the warm, miniature hurricane of pleasure from the other. Across the table, Arkady's eyes gleamed at her mockingly. He was showing her that he was in command and she could almost see him flexing his muscles while the approval on one hand and the disapproval on the other was treated with the same bland indifference. And he could escape the consequences—Joanna watched him remove himself from the table at the end of the meal and go off to his small room, and she watched Anna hurrying after him with a tray of coffee and the brandy. Zeus had announced his decision, and if lesser mortals wanted to squabble about it, that was their business—Arkady was behaving in a thoroughly omnipotent manner!

Kore went off as well—to the kitchen, to Joanna's surprise, where she could be heard clashing plates and cutlery about. Joanna shrugged. Kore was demonstrating as well that—

when everything suited her she could be obliging and thoughtful. As for herself, Joanna's flight to the bedroom was halted by Ilone's hand on her arm and her vague excuse of looking in on Dion to see that he was quite safe and well was brushed aside.

'As if he could get up and run away!' There was a nasty gleam in Ilone's dark eyes and her fingers tightened on Joanna's wrist until they felt like a manacle. 'And if he was crying,' the Greek woman went on, 'I think we'd have heard him, don't you?

'I compliment you, Joanna,' Ilone seated herself in a high-backed chair close to the fireplace full of blazing logs. 'In the few weeks you have been here, you have regained most of the ground you lost when you ran away.' She was neat and precise and very, very cool, which could be dangerous. 'Of course,' she continued, 'your child is a boy, which has given you an enormous advantage. Do sit down, we need to talk.'

'Do we?' For the first time, Joanna regretted not smoking—at moments like this, it was something which would have occupied her hands. Her eyes slid round the room and lighted on a bottle of wine on the table, nearly two thirds full. Without seeming to hurry, she strode across to it, examined the label—a Naoussa from Macedonia, unresinated—and with cold fingers she poured herself a glassful. The idea was in her head that she was going to need something, maybe alcohol would fill the bill. 'Talk away, then,' she said shortly as she came back to the fire and dragged a chair up to sit in it. 'And I hope you'll excuse me if I don't say much. It's been a very long day and I'm rather tired. You do the talking, Ilone; I'm sure you have so much to say, and I'll just sit and listen.'

'Very well,' the Greek woman shrugged gracefully. 'The point is, where to begin . . .'

'At the beginning,' Joanna prompted helpfully. 'That's where all the best stories start. Then they go on, right through to the end, and stop. I hope it won't be a very long story—I've already warned you, I'm very tired.' From beneath her drooped eyelids, she watched Ilone's face, caught the tightening of her lovely mouth and heard the muffled sniff of exasperation. 'Keep it up, Joanna,' she advised herself silently, 'and don't be foolish, don't lose your temper.'

'I believe I have you to thank for upsetting my arrangements for Kore.' Ilone set the ball rolling, her dark eyes full of an icy anger which was almost frustration, and Joanna took a sip of her wine and shook her head.

'Not me,' she denied. 'Arkady, maybe, and possibly Kore herself, but definitely not me! Although I heartily approve of the change in plan. I haven't seen young Serghios recently, of course; perhaps he's improved of late, but based on my recollections of him, he *was* rather offputting, hardly a Greek god.'

'Which is just the point I'm trying to make.' Ilone was keeping her temper beautifully. 'A husband isn't chosen for a girl simply because of his looks, there are a great many other considerations, and the girl's parents . . .'

'But you're not,' Joanna interrupted softly. 'Not Kore's parent.'

'That has nothing to do with it!' Ilone forgot herself for a second and snapped, her little white teeth biting off the words. 'An arrangement, a long-standing arrangement, has been cancelled, and I blame you. Until you came back, Kore was perfectly happy with the future which had been arranged for her.'

'And if you believe that, you'll believe anything!' Joanna heard herself getting heated and tried to cool down. 'The girl was unhappy about it.'

'And I blame you for that as well,' Ilone pursed her mouth into an expression of distaste. 'Before you came here, she accepted it. After all, Greek fathers have been finding suitable husbands for their daughters for hundreds of years, it's the way things are done here, among our class of people.'

'You buy the best you can afford, you mean.' Joanna echoed Ilone's distaste. 'Poor things, sold off to a life of standing in the background and being a superior sort of servant. I pity them! And having to sit at home, bearing and rearing children, while their husbands flit from one pillow friend to the next. If I were Kore's mother, I'd want something better than that for her.'

'But you are not her mother,' Ilone pointed out sweetly, and Joanna snapped back:

'Neither are you!'

It silenced Ilone temporarily, but not for long. Joanna sat silent and had the impression that she could see the cogs meshing and the wheels turning in Ilone's brain. It was a tenacious kind of brain, she thought, but not needle-sharp—once thrown out of gear, it took a little while to get started again.

'All this is pointless.' The Greek woman made a moue of displeasure as she fiddled with the clasp of her handbag, a delicate thing of silk-embroidered fine leather, too thin to contain much beside a handkerchief, compact and lipstick.

'Arkady has changed his mind and his decision is final, much as I dislike it, so we will abandon the subject of Kore and speak about you.'

'Me?' Joanna raised her eyebrows. 'Don't tell me you've got plans for me?'

'No,' Ilone was very serious, 'but for a long while, I've thought you weren't happy. You conceal it well, but it's there, in your eyes.' She snapped open the bag and withdrew something that gleamed blue and gold in the firelight. 'I thought this might make you happier.'

'Thank you,' Joanna accepted the passport gravely, turning it over and over between her fingers, making a little grimace at the sight of the four-year-old picture of herself. Was it possible that a woman's appearance could change so much in so short a time, or could it be that the twenty-one-year-old girl pictured there no longer existed; that the twenty-five-year-old woman was a completely different person?

'May I ask how you got this?' she asked. 'Or is it one of those things it would be better not to question?'

'Much better not to question,' Ilone waved it aside with a look of hauteur. 'Sometimes the truth can be very wounding.'

Joanne wondered if that was supposed to mean that the Greek woman had been asked to give it to her. That would have been quite like Arkady, but on the other hand, it would also be quite like him to toss the passport into an unlocked drawer of his desk, knowing it would be useless to her. Quietly she extended the booklet, admiring the steadiness of her hand.

'Put it back, please,' she said quietly. This time

she wasn't going to lose her temper and start shouting—this time she would be as dignified and cool as her opponent. 'You see,' she said gravely but with a wry twist to her mouth, 'it's no good to me, not on its own.' She watched as Ilone's hand went into the bag again and caught a glimpse of a thin wad of Greek notes. 'No, I don't mean I need money, so please don't insult me by offering any. It's just that the passport is useless without Dion's papers. If I leave, I would take him with me, and if I can't do that then we both stay. He's one of the important things in my life, too important for me to abandon him.'

Ilone made no attempt to take the passport, so Joanna stood up, walked the few paces that separated them and tossed it down into her silken lap.

'I don't know if you're playing Arkady's game or your own,' she continued softly. 'It could be either, I've no means of telling, but one thing I'm certain of—my son and I go or stay, together. Good night!'

She felt deathly tired whcn she reached the bedroom, and a swift glance in the mirror told her she looked it, but it wasn't a physical tiredness but a mental one—she felt as though she no longer had the energy to fight. Arkady was already there, in bed, with Dion propped up against his raised knees, and man and child were staring at each other consideringly.

'I'm keeping him quiet for you.' Arkady slanted her a glance that told her nothing—it was impossible for her to tell whether he had instigated the passport business or not.

'Keep him quiet a bit longer,' she suggested

drily. 'Tell him the story of your life while I get ready for bed. Who knows, he might find it interesting!'

She was beginning to wish she hadn't behaved so well. At least in a good shouting match there was generally a victor and the vanquished, but the polite war of words she had just had with Ilone was a sterile thing—it gave her no satisfaction and left her with one more question than she had had when she started. Nobody had won or lost anything, and the status was still very much quo.

CHAPTER NINE

SYLVIE was wearing an oversized apron that came nearly to her ankles and completely eclipsed the pink and white stripes of her dress and Anna had fixed her up with a mobcap to match, so that the child looked like a Victorian rag doll. Nothing was to be seen of her except her mouth and chin and two small black boots at the nether end. But she had a quiet air of contentment that oozed out and spread over everything as she pattered about the bedroom.

Dion, for once, was not being good. Fed full, bathed and changed, he refused to return quietly to his crib. Each effort to put him there resulted in howls of wrath and a red face out of which his rapidly darkening eyes glared angrily.

'He is not ill,' Sylvie gave it as her expert opinion. 'I will take him down to the patio and put him in his pram, *kyria*. There he may see things. It is quite warm and not raining and he may watch the trees.' Without waiting for a yea or nay, she humped the baby on to her almost non-existent hip, where he suddenly stopped yelling, and toddled off with him, the huge frill round her mobcap bobbing and the over-large apron crackling starchily around her thin ankles.

Left to herself, Joanna breathed a sigh of relief and dismissed every fantasy that had fled through her mind—thoughts of fevers and terminal, painful illnesses sank back into her subconscious and she set about small chores to get the room ready for the cleaning woman whom she could hear operating downstairs. The aroma of fresh coffee and hot new bread wafted up to her, making her mouth water, and when the last piece of soiled clothing had been rammed into the linen basket, she hurried downstairs, only to be stopped halfway by another piercing yell and the sound of angry voices.

Not Dion—the patio was quiet and the noise was coming from upstairs; Kore and somebody having a real 'cat in the alley' fight. Joanna shrugged—it had nothing to do with her—and continued on downwards, only to halt as another yell split the peace, followed by an angry altercation. It was all in Greek, quite incomprehensible, but it sounded ominous. Kore and—she listened, caught the timbre of the other voice—Kore and Ilone were going at it hammer and tongs. Joanna's mouth curled into a smile. Kore and her father shared the same temper, but Arkady controlled his; his daughter hadn't learned to do that yet, but she would, given time— Joanna's foot hovered over the next downward stair, coffee and rolls were drawing her towards the kitchen, when the crash and tinkle of glass shattering stopped her abruptly.

Flying glass, and Dion was right underneath them, on the patio. He could be hurt, scarred for life, and she turned and fled back up the stairs. Her knock on Kore's door was a mere formality, the door was opening under her hand when she tapped and hurried into the bedroom with a white face and angry eyes.

'What the hell's going on?' she demanded,

raising her voice to be heard above Ilone's angry scolding and Kore's shrill little yells. She kicked at the splintered remains of a crystal bowl. 'Who threw that? Dion's down on the patio, you could have killed him or marked him for life!' And then she spoiled it all with an hysterical giggle. Ilone's nightdress and negligee were straight out of the Folies Bergère, circa 1935—yards and yards of oyster satin embellished with about a ton of lace— did Arkady like that sort of thing? because if so, she'd buy some, but not with a sweeping train, although the train had its advantages. As Ilone swung round on the intruder, the weight of it pulled the cut-on-the-cross satin against her, outlining every curve of her body.

'This is what's going on!' Ilone was the first to recover and she waved a large brown envelope under Joanna's nose. 'This! It was delivered by hand early this morning, and it shows what all this modern freedom for girls leads to. This——' she used a Greek word Joanna hadn't ever heard and didn't know the meaning of, but it sounded shocking, and Kore's high-pitched mew of anger confirmed her suspicion.

In contrast to Ilone, Kore was fully dressed in a tee-shirt and jeans, but she was huddled on the bed, unrepentant and incredibly angry. The stream of Greek coming from her lips sounded as bad, if not worse, than Ilone's single word, but it was definitely a denial of some sort. The envelope continued to wave under Joanna's nose, and without thinking, she grasped at it, wrenched it from the Greek woman's hand and turned it over, registering that it had been opened and that it was addressed to Kore.

Joanna lifted her nose as though there was a bad smell somewhere. 'You make a habit of opening things addressed to other people?' she enquired snootily, but Ilone didn't look one bit ashamed, instead she looked triumphant.

'I opened it because I knew what was in it,' she said maliciously. 'If I had given the envelope to Kore, she would have destroyed it unopened, because she knows what it contains. I have heard whispers of unrest in Paleo this year, and always it has been the same thing. Arkady shall see this, and he will perhaps realise I was right when I told him he was allowing his daughter too much freedom. Kore has behaved very badly and she must be punished for it. I shall see she is punished . . .'

'You'll do nothing of the kind!' Joanna had not so much come to a decision, it was more as if the decision had been thrust on her. 'Not before I know what all this is about, and punishment, if it's deserved, will come from Kore's father. You'll have no say in it!'

'Oh, there *will* be punishment.' Ilone's voice held a trace of almost sadistic enjoyment. 'Open the envelope and see for yourself!'

'May I?' Joanna raised an eyebrow at Kore, making a show of politeness, and the girl raised a tear-streaked face to nod.

'But it can't be me,' she muttered defiantly. 'I wouldn't do anything like that. I told Hank I wouldn't pose for him. He must have taken it without my knowing——'

Joanna kept her face masklike and strictly professional as she glanced down at the photograph. A good photo, the work of an expert, not only in the taking of it but in the printing as well. The background had been deliberately fogged out a bit so that the back view of the nude girl stood out clearly. She had often seen worse but not often better work, on eight-by-ten matt paper—it was good enough to hold its own in an exhibition.

With a little sigh, she slipped the photograph back into the envelope and dropped it on the bottom of Kore's bed. 'I'll look at it more closely later—but meanwhile,' she raised a hand to halt Ilone's threatened outburst, 'I don't want anything said about this. Now, leave us alone, Ilone. Kore and I have some talking to do, and since it doesn't concern you, you needn't stay for it.'

'It does concern me,' Ilone snapped back. 'Kore is my . . .'

'Spare me the family tree,' Joanna interrupted rudely, and took a firm pace towards the other woman, her eyes very bright and battle flags flying in her cheeks. 'Out!' she said briefly, and as the door was closing behind Ilone's trailing satin and lace she turned back to Kore.

'Your father's gone to Paxos?' and at Kore's almost imperceptible shrug, 'Don't you know?'

Kore shook her head. 'I haven't seen him this morning. I did ask Anna, but she isn't sure where he's gone—maybe Paxos, maybe Kerkira or even Athens, he didn't say—he didn't even say when he'd be back.'

'Greek men and their damn business!' Joanna choked back a rude word. 'Sometimes I think they live in a world all of their own. This photo——' she touched the envelope reluctantly as though it was contaminated, 'it's going to make him mad, you know that. Lord, he made enough fuss when you appeared yesterday in that bikini!'

'It's the result of the Turkish occupation.' Kore was recovering. 'It lasted a long time, you know. Even after so long, nearly a hundred years—haven't you noticed?—how some men still wear Turkish trousers, the sort that button up at the back, and how the old women always have their hair covered? Couldn't we burn it, Joanna?'

'No point.' Joanna nibbled at a fingernail. 'It's no use burning a print if Hank Sommers still has the negative.' She reached for the envelope to draw out the photo and examine it closely. 'I don't think he's had this printed at the *fotografion*, the background's not really out of focus, it's been fogged out—he'd have to do that himself...'

'He does.' Kore looked surprised at Joanna's ignorance. 'He has a darkroom.'

'Where?'

'Down at the taverna where he lives, of course. He has two rooms—well, not two rooms, exactly. He has a bedroom and a little place where there's a hand basin and things. I saw it once while I was waiting for him—that was the day he asked me to go to bed with him. He was angry when I told him I didn't want to.'

Joanna shook her head in bewilderment. 'There are times, my girl, when I think you're as old as sin. Now listen, Kore. I'm going down to Paleokastritsa, and if I get a chance, I'll raid that darkroom and find the negative, and if I do, we can forget all about it—your father need never know. But if I'm not successful, I'm afraid you'll have to tell him yourself and hope he understands.'

Back in the bedroom, Joanna had another think. She would need an excuse to get into Hank's lodgings. Her eyes lighted on the case containing the floods and stands—that would do, and if she carried it off with a high hand, chucked her weight about a bit ...

When she came downstairs again with the case in her hand, Kore was waiting for her at the bottom of the outside staircase and the beach buggy was standing ready for her to drive away.

'I know you're in a hurry, Jo, but there's something I have to tell you. I'll come with you as far as Krini so I won't make you late, and I can tell you as we drive along.'

'More misdeeds?' Joanna started the engine and watched as her stepdaughter scrambled in beside her. 'Very well, but keep it short. What else is there?'

'Lies.' Out of the corner of her eye, Joanna saw a tear drip down Kore's cheek. 'I was so miserable, Jo. You and Papa, and he didn't seem to love me as much any more, not after he married you. I was jealous and I used to do awful things just to make somebody notice me.' She gave a sadly rueful little laugh. 'Remember that boat boy, Jo—the one I was going to run away with, and how you stopped me? I lied to you that day. I've tried to pretend it never happened, but I know it did, and it's better you know the truth about me—I don't think I'm a very nice person.'

'Just about average.' Joanna kept it light, she was driving and she had to keep her mind on what passed for a road. 'What lies?'

'About Papa and Ilone.' Kore gulped distinctly, Joanna heard her. 'Not about Ilone not being able to have any babies—that was the truth, everybody knows that, but it wasn't true, what I said about them being lovers. That was just a story I made up for myself, and I used to think I'd tell you and you'd go away and Papa would forget you and everything would be all right again. But inside, I knew it wasn't a good story and you wouldn't believe me—it was only when I got really cross that I told you. But you didn't believe me—I knew you wouldn't, I mean, you couldn't believe a thing like that about Papa, nobody could. I got it out of a magazine, you know; one of Ilone's. You didn't believe me, did you?'

'Not a word.' Joanna kept it cheerful. 'I used to make up stories when,' she had been going to say 'when I was a child' but hastily changed it to, 'when I was your age. Most youngsters do when they're growing up. You're nothing out of the ordinary.' And she silently echoed Kore's sigh of relief with one of her own. All that mattered was that Kore shouldn't be made to feel guilty, and she summoned up a cheerful smile. 'It was a good story, of course, and you told it very well, but it didn't fit the facts so I couldn't believe it, could I? Here's where I drop you off.' She slowed the buggy to a halt and watched as Kore skipped out and stood waving as she drove away.

Joanna chided herself for being over-scrupulous. She could have done with Kore's company, but on the other hand, if anything went wrong it would be disastrous to have the girl with her—she went over her plan again, and then speculated on what she would do if Hank Sommers should be at the taverna when she arrived there. It was a thought that had just occurred to her—all her preparations, even to the roll of unexposed film which she'd stuffed in her bag and which she intended to use as an excuse to get into his darkroom, had been based on the supposition that he would be away somewhere.

And if he wasn't—unconsciously, Joanna bit her lip—she would just have to threaten him with Arkady and a bit of physical violence. The buggy hit a pothole and the jerk of it made her clenched teeth bite into her lip so that she could taste warm blood in her mouth. After that, she stopped thinking and concentrated on getting to Paleokastritsa in one piece.

She put the buggy in a car park belonging to a hotel; it wouldn't be wise to leave it outside the taverna—the dratted thing was too distinctive— and wandered off, trying to give the appearance of a woman with plenty of time to spare. The long case containing the collapsible stands, the reflectors and flood bulbs rather spoiled the picture, but she tried to overcome it by idling along and taking a little time to look in the souvenir shop windows. A lot of them were still open for the benefit of the winter visitors, although they weren't doing a lot of trade. And at last she wandered into the taverna with a negligent 'Kalimera' to the proprietor, wondering if he knew who she was or if he thought she was one of the tourists.

'Coffee, please,' she said in an exhausted tone, but by this time she was feeling exhausted. 'Nescafé,' she stipulated as an afterthought—her mouth was already dry, and if it got filled up with coffee grounds she wouldn't be able to get a word out—and she sat, trying to look bored to tears, until he came back with the tray.

'*Kyrie,*' she gulped nervously, 'I've come to see the Kyrios Sommers. Would you tell him I'm here?'

'Excuse,' the proprietor shook his head sadly as if he was announcing a catastrophe and wiped up the few drops she had spilled on the plastic-covered tablecloth—her hand was shaking so much she wondered how she hadn't spilled the lot. 'The Kyrios Sommers is not here, *kyria*. Today, he has gone with a coachful of visitors on a small tour— Kerkira, the palace and gardens and then to Kassiopi. He will return this evening, I think.'

'Oh dear!' Joanna covered her relief with a worried look. 'The Kyrios was going to let me use his darkroom,' she felt in her bag and produced a roll of film—a used cassette looked very much like an unused one and she hoped he wouldn't notice the telltale end of film showing. 'But I don't suppose he'll mind if I use it while he's not here— if you'd show me the way ...?' She saw the uncertainty on the proprietor's very mobile face and hurried on. 'I shan't be long, I just want one print. I mustn't be long, my husband, the Kyrios Arkady St. Vlastos, will be calling for me soon. If I'm not finished when he arrives, will you ask him to wait for me, please, and while I'm here, I can return some equipment the Kyrios Sommers lent me.' She nudged the long case with her foot. 'I'd rather leave it in his rooms, the contents are very fragile.'

Joanna held her breath and waited, surreptitiously crossing her fingers and praying hard. If nobody much knew her, everybody would know Arkady and be aware that he had an English wife—she prayed again that the proprietor, knowing her to be English, would merely accept her very unusual request as one of those odd things the English did, like preferring Nescafé to proper coffee and going green when they were offered squid to eat. 'If you would show me the way,' she repeated faintly but firmly to add, 'and if you would carry this case for me?'

It worked! The proprietor's face had relaxed into a smile and he was picking up the case, so Joanna abandoned her coffee to follow him as swiftly as possible, before he had a change of mind.

Hank Sommers' lodgings were neat, clean and very basic. The bedsitting room contained the bare necessities, a bed, chair, table, a wardrobe and a large amount of shelving along one wall which was filled to overflowing with books, magazines and a great deal of other clutter. The small room that led off it, he had improved on. There was no window and what had originally been a simple wash place was now a reasonably equipped darkroom. A long but narrow old kitchen table, probably a throwout from the taverna, stood along one wall and held an enlarger. Plastic dishes, stained but clean, were stacked tidily and a home-made shelf held bottles of chemicals and plastic containers of prepared solutions.

There were a couple of shallow drawers in the table, and Joanna gravitated towards them as though drawn by a magnet. One held a thermometer and paper, the latter in black lightproof plastic bags and boxed according to size while the other contained plastic tongs, several other small pieces of equipment, a few light bulbs, both red and clear, and a spare set of lenses for the enlarger.

Over the washbasin another shelf had been set up, holding measuring cylinders and a big developing tank, and attached to it was a string line, evidently used for drying—a couple of prints were still clipped to it, and she inspected them. Both were quite innocuous, studies of the wrinkled face of an old fisherman, and she chided herself for expecting anything else. These rooms would be cleaned every day, and Hank Sommers wasn't the sort of fool who would leave doubtful pictures for just anybody to see. His negatives would be hidden, of course, and—she looked round the purely functional darkroom—there was nowhere here to hide anything.

She glanced at her watch—she still had plenty of time, more than an hour and a half, allowing for the journey back to the villa. Whatever she hoped to find *must* be hidden somewhere in the bedsitting room, and with a sigh of despair she went back to it—This wasn't going to be so easy, but if she went at it systematically . . .

A tap at the door sent her scurrying back into the darkroom, where she hastily switched on the overhead red light and then came out to open the door, pretending to blink a bit and wiping her quite dry hands on a towel. But it was only the proprietor with another pot of Nescafé and a cup and saucer on a tray.

'The Kyrios Sommers always called for coffee while he was working,' the man beamed at her, and she forced a grateful smile in return. 'You have finished, *kyria*?'

'Not yet, but I shan't be long.' The man followed her in, put the tray on the table and moved towards the door of the darkroom.

'No!' It burst from her lips and he halted with his hand on the latch. 'I've got a couple of prints in the dish, developing,' she said hastily. 'They'll spoil if the light gets to them and I haven't time to do any more, so please don't open that door. Thank you for the coffee.' She hurried past him and slid through the narrowest opening she could manage. 'They're due out now,' she gasped, 'and thank you for the coffee. You won't forget to tell my husband when he comes, will you?'

When she heard his footsteps going back down the stairs, she eased herself back into the bedsit and poured herself coffee with hands that were far from steady. She was as nervous as a cat, and over and over in her mind was running that stupid quotation '. . . a tangled web we weave when first we practise to deceive'. That was a laugh for a start! Did it mean it got easier with practice—the web became less tangled the oftener one deceived, because if that was so, she wished she'd passed a lifetime spent solely in deception—she wouldn't be shaking like a leaf and wishing she'd never got herself involved!

The coffee seemed to calm her down and she gulped at it gratefully. Now for this room—the bed first. People were always supposed to hide things under mattresses or pillows.

But not in this case—Joanna let the mattress fall back on to the wooden slats that took the place of a spring—she also plumped up the pillows and straightened the spread before turning her attention to the wardrobe. It was vast and almost empty, although there was room enough in it to hide an elephant—which just left the shelving, and she groaned as she looked at its ordered chaos.

Be systematic, she told herself, start at the beginning—and she did, with a pile of magazines. Halfway through the pile, she came on a big envelope containing seven or eight loose pages, and she drew them out with eager fingers, but there was nothing else in the envelope, no negatives. The pages, doubled over to go in the envelope, opened in her hand, and she gasped; if not negatives, she'd got something—all nudes and all very artistic, and Hank had been given the credit—his name was in small print at the bottom of each picture—his contributions to the magazines, she supposed, taken out and saved as souvenirs.

She put the envelope and its contents on one side and continued burrowing, rather like a frantic rabbit. Another envelope came to light a bit further down the pile, a smaller envelope, and this time she was in luck. As she opened it, negatives came sliding out—strips of three each in a transparent cover. Her mouth curved in triumph—she'd been right after all. These were thirty-five-millimetre negatives, that Rolliecon *was* a blind; for serious work like this, Hank used a much better camera.

Not that there was anything wrong with the Rolliecon, it was a good camera, but its proper place was firmly fixed on to a good stout tripod and its shutter operated with a cable release so that there would be no chance of camera shake. One by one, she held the strips of negatives to the light—all nudes, or nearly so, and all taken here on Corfu, and Kore's was among them. Joanna felt almost sick with relief.

One last chore—and that was to search for more

prints. It wouldn't do any good to destroy these negatives if there was a print left from which a copy could be photographed, and she settled grimly to the task. It took her another half hour to complete her search of the shelving—she found another envelope with some prints in it, but she went on doggedly until she was quite sure there were no others.

The negatives she put safely in her handbag, but before she started in on her destruction she took another look at the prints. They were absolutely lovely, the best work she had ever seen, and as far as she could judge, none of the girls, including Kore, had known they were being photographed. There was a careless grace about them that could only come from complete unawareness. It was a shame to have to destroy such work, but it had to be done. Nude models were one thing, they knew what they were doing, but these girls—that was a different matter. Teenagers, members of good Greek families—girls whose fathers wouldn't hesitate to beat them if they ever found out. Suddenly the prints lost all their charm and became revolting, so much so that Joanna had to hold them gingerly by the corners and between just one finger and thumb as if they were infectious, and she pattered back into the darkroom with them. In there she had seen a metal waste bin and it would be a good thing to contain the funeral pyre.

The little cheap cigarette lighter with which she had come provided failed to light the first time, but she flicked the wheel again and the jet of gas sprang into flame. One by one, she touched it to the corners of the photos, dropping each one singly into the bin as it caught fire and counting as the dropped them. There mustn't be anything left except ashes, and when the prints were gone, she'd start on the negatives.

As she dropped the last photo into the bin, the darkroom door opened and she whirled round with an excuse bubbling up on to her tongue, but it wasn't the proprietor, it was Arkady standing there with one eyebrow raised and his mouth curved into a smile.

'What are you doing, *agape*?'

'Burning the place down,' she snapped, relief— although why she should feel relieved, she didn't know—making her angry. 'And what are *you* doing here?'

'You left a message for me with Spiros.' He lounged against the frame of the door, his eyes never leaving her face.

'S-Spiros?'

'The proprietor,' he exclaimed gravely. 'I was passing and he called me over. Is this a favourite place of yours? You seem to be here quite frequently.'

'They serve Nescafé,' she muttered on a defiant note, then went on the attack. 'And what are you doing here?' she repeated the question. 'Can't you ever let anybody know where you'll be at any given time? I wake up in the morning and you've gone—you're like the invisible man. Nobody knows where you are because you haven't bothered to say where you've gone or when you'll be back . . .'

'I went down to Kerkira.' He sounded quite patient. 'I intended to be back before you woke and I didn't want to wake you before I went because I knew Dion had you up early. I was being thoughtful.'

'That's a turn-up for the book!' she snapped savagely.

'But when haven't I been thoughtful?' Again, a dark eyebrow flew up. 'Have you ever had less than tender, loving care from me?'

'Ha! Threats!' Joanna swung on her heel so that her back was towards him—it was surprising how anger could grow, almost out of nothing. It started as a tiny niggle, she'd encouraged it to cover her uncertainty, and now it was almost out of control and was making her unreasonable. She swallowed the lump of it in her throat and asked, carefully so that she didn't sound too interested:

'You've come here straight from Kerkira?'

'No.' He must have left the doorway, because she could feel his warm breath on the back of her neck. 'I went straight home.'

'Oh!'

'Yes—oh! What have you been up to, *gineka mou*? I left a quiet, peaceful house this morning and I found a disaster area when I returned—Anna throwing things about in the kitchen, both Kore and Ilone locked in their bedrooms—the only normality was in little Sylvie, who was playing on a rug on the patio with Dion.'

'Oh!'

'Is that all you can say, Joanna?' he asked, and when she refused to answer, 'Will it help at all if I tell you I waited and Kore finally emerged with a very garbled story—something about nobody ever believing her and you going off into battle. A photograph featured largely, but she couldn't show me because you'd taken it with you, and I gathered, from what she said, that it had something to do with Hank Sommers. She implored me to come *at once* to save you . . .'

'*You* save *me*?' Joanna was indignantly wrathful. 'I came here to save Kore—and you!' she added, and dodging past him, she hurried into the bedsit. 'Come and see what I've found!' she shouted over her shoulder as she started a search among the pile of magazines for the envelope containing the pictures, the envelope she had so carefully replaced because it hadn't been what she was looking for.

'See these!' She unfolded the sheets and spread them under Arkady's nose, and at his look of distaste, 'What's the matter, don't they turn you on? They're supposed to. They're what's known as centrefolds and they're one of the main attractions in men's magazines. If they don't make you light up like a Christmas tree there must be something wrong with your hormones . . .'

'Stop it,' Joanna!' he broke in on her biting sarcasm, and she fell silent to watch as he flicked through the sheets before tossing them down on to the table and wiping his fingers as if they had touched something unpleasant. 'There's nothing wrong with my hormones, and I don't have to fantasise, you know that!'

Joanna had the grace to blush and then returned to the attack. 'You don't understand,' she stormed. 'Hank Sommers doesn't fantasise either, he takes that sort of photograph; those are some he's taken and had published, you can see the credit in small print under each one. And he doesn't use models, like any decent photographer. He's a Peeping Tom. He may be good at his job, I don't dispute that, but he's a louse!'

She paused, undecided how to continue. It all depended on how much Arkady knew—how much Kore had told him. There would be no sense or kindness in involving his daughter if it wasn't absolutely necessary—she would spare him that if she could.

'Shouldn't we be getting out of here?' she asked hesitantly. 'I mean, the proprietor was very kind and obliging to let me come up here. I wasn't exactly truthful—I said Hank had given me permission, but I think we ought to get out before he comes back.'

'No.' Arkady had planted himself in the middle of the floor and looked as if he was set for a long stay. His face was rock-hard and his eyes, when they met hers, were unfathomable. 'We stay, Joanna, until I get the truth, and if I can't get it out of you, we'll wait until Sommers arrives and I'll get it from him!'

'We can't stay—at least, I can't stay,' she seized on her only excuse. 'I have to get back to Dion ...' She caught up her bag and attempted to pass Arkady to get to the door, but his hand caught her about the waist and held her firmly.

'The truth, Joanna,' he insisted. 'You wouldn't come down here, lie your way into a man's lodgings, search the place and burn things without a very good reason, and I want to know what that reason is, so we stay here until you tell me.'

'No!' she protested, almost fighting him, and then went rigid at the sound of footsteps on the stairs. Then the door was flung ajar and Hank Sommers stood in the opening.

CHAPTER TEN

'WELL, this is a real pleasure,' Hank smiled broadly as he strode forward with a look of delight on his open, ingenuous face. 'Spiros told me I had visitors, but I didn't expect it to be you. I told him to send up a bottle of ouzo and some glasses, but,' he smiled at Joanna, 'I guess you'd like something different, ma'am?'

Joanna worried about that smile, it looked genuine enough, but it didn't seem to reach his eyes—although that could be her inbuilt bias working. 'Thank you,' she said quietly, 'but it's not necessary. I brought back your floods,' she nodded at the case which she had dropped by the table, 'and I—that is, we wanted to thank you personally . . .' Her voice died away as she realised Hank wasn't listening to her. All his attention was on the centrefolds which Arkady had tossed down on the table, and she caught his swift glance at the stack of magazines on the shelving.

'You people been looking at some of my work?' He didn't seem disturbed, in fact he looked rather pleased—as if he would have shown them himself, given the slightest encouragement. 'They're real good, don't you think?'

'My wife,' Arkady broke the little silence that followed the question, 'my wife pointed out to me that the technique and composition were better than she had expected, but then she supposed you to be an amateur. Now, it seems, you are a professional and

169

she is less enthusiastic—mainly, I think, because you don't use models who are as professional as yourself.'

Joanna had been keeping her eyes on Hank's face, and the change in his expression shocked her. The wide, careless smile was gone and his features now matched his eyes—cold, calculating and faintly malicious. As she watched, the malice grew and he deliberately looked at the stacked magazines; he even edged a little nearer to them.

'I guess you've been prying, ma'am,' he reproved her cynically, and Joanna suddenly became afraid. This young man wasn't the type to go down by himself, he would drag others down with him and not care how many people were hurt. He was running his fingers down the spines of the magazines, unerringly reaching the place where the envelope of prints had been hidden. His finger slid between and was removed.

'Yes, definitely prying, ma'am,' and unwittingly—and she couldn't blame him because he didn't know—Arkady made it easy for Hank.

'My wife arrived here a little while before me. I'm afraid she found some samples of your work and decided they were unacceptable; I believe she's burned them. She had quite a fire going in the waste bin in your darkroom when I arrived. Needless to say, I applaud her action.'

'You burned my prints, ma'am?' And as Joanna nodded firmly she saw the malice increase. 'Now that is a shame. I reckoned those prints were about the best I'd ever done, especially the one of Kore. I guess I don't have to look for the negatives . . .? No, I reckon not,' he answered his own question. 'Like me, ma'am, you're a professional, you'd know what to look for and what to destroy. But it

surely was a pleasure taking those photographs
. . .' But his words fell on deaf ears. Joanna had
been praying for a miracle ever since Hank had
come through the door, and as she walked across
to the long window that opened on to a small balcony, the miracle came—or was it no miracle but
just that her senses were made a little more acute
by stress and she was seeing things more clearly?

Whatever it was, it hit her like a thunderbolt,
driving out fear so that she could be quite calm. In
the calmness she could hear Arkady, very polite,
very precise; his English so elegant and old-
fashioned it made her smile, although she could
almost feel the pain Hank's revelation was causing
her husband. She looked at him, at his dark,
enigmatic face, and drew comfort from it. Nothing
showed, not anger or hurt.

'My wife, whose opinion I value in this matter,'
he was saying, 'tells me that the photographs of
which you were so proud were all taken without
either the knowledge or consent of the subjects.
Am I correct, *agape*?'

'Yes,' she gave him a small smile. 'And from
here, I think,' she tapped the floor with the toe of
her shoe, 'there's a clear view of part of the beach,
and it's not so far away—a good stout tripod, a
telephoto lens, a couple of young girls going for a
very early morning swim, some fast film to freeze
the movement—it would be easy.'

'That camera?' Arkady indicated the Rolliecon
still hanging from Hank's shoulder as though he
would like to smash it to pieces.

'Oh no,' now she could really smile and the
amusement crept into her eyes, 'leave him that
one, Arkady, it's too old, it isn't versatile enough

for his "serious" work. He'll have a much better one somewhere,' and when Hank attempted to speak, she swung on him, silencing him with a glare. 'I've seen the negatives,' she spat at him. 'They're the wrong size for that.' She turned back to Arkady. 'I expect he has it all in the boot of his car. He's supposed to be conducting a tour round the town and then on to Kassiopi, but perhaps he's having a day off instead to get on with his real work and he'd need his equipment for that!'

'You've a nasty way of putting things, ma'am,' Hank seized his opportunity when she ran out of breath. 'We all have to make a living, and I've been noticing how tight you're holding that bag—I don't think you've burned those negs at all, so I reckon I'll just have them back. They're my property, ma'am.'

Joanna didn't scurry, but she was extremely quick to take shelter behind her husband's substantial form, to hold her bag tightly and let Arkady do the fighting for her.

'Didn't you?' He looked down at her severely.

'No time,' she explained briefly. 'You came in just as I'd finished with the prints. I was going to get rid of the negatives separately, they flare a bit and I didn't want to set the place on fire.'

'Give.' He held out his hand, but she shook her head.

'No, Arkady, you can't let him have them—he can take off another load of prints. It will have been all for nothing . . .'

'He isn't going to have them.' Arkady pulled the ashtray towards him. 'He's going to have the doubtful pleasure of seeing them go up in smoke, and I'm going to have the real pleasure of watching his face while they burn.' He had his lighter ready, and she handed over the small packet. She had always known that Arkady's hands were graceful, and now she could admire their dexterity as they slid the negatives from the envelope and touched the flame to the corner of each strip. He let each one flare and die before he started on the next.

It didn't take long, and when the ashtray contained nothing but a charred, sticky mess, he tucked his hand beneath her elbow and drew her towards the door, stilling Hank Sommers' protest with a curt wave of his hand.

'Yes, I'm well aware that both my wife and I are guilty of invading your privacy and destroying some of your property, but I don't think you should worry about it. I can't speak for the rest of the world, but for this one small island I can, and I tell you, you're no longer welcome. I advise you to leave as soon as possible. Spiros, who has been my friend since we were children, has suddenly discovered he needs this room for another tenant who is arriving tomorrow morning, and I feel sure you won't be able to find alternative accommodation, so I will arrange a room for you in Kerkira for tonight—but only tonight. But don't delay your departure beyond tomorrow—these small islands can be very treacherous and I wouldn't wish you to suffer an unpleasant accident.'

Joanna looked up swiftly and saw that Arkady's face wore exactly the same expression as when he had come to her London place and forced her to return to Corfu. He was threatening—in a very nice way, of course, but it wasn't an idle threat, he meant every word of it. Further thought was impossible as he pushed her through the door and down the stairs.

'Go and wait in the car while I speak to Spiros,' and when she opened her mouth to object, 'That is an order, *gineka mou*.'

'. . . but the buggy,' she gasped. 'It's in the hotel parking . . .'

'It will be fetched—now do as I say,' he instructed her out of the corner of his mouth. 'Go! The rest is man's business and women have no part in it.'

Joanna kept a dignified, almost sulky silence for the first mile of the journey back to the villa, but she couldn't keep it up for ever.

'You meant what you said about accidents?'

'Of course,' Arkady nodded serenely without taking his eyes off the road. 'They happen. The strongest swimmer can drown, the roads on this island can be very treacherous. I meant it, my dear.'

Joanna collapsed back in her seat and looked at her watch. 'I'm late,' she announced almost with triumph. 'Dion will be screaming his head off, and it's all your fault. If you'd left me alone, not interfered, I'd have finished and been away from the taverna before Hank came back. Which would have saved all that unpleasantness.'

'And left him free to do the same thing again,' he pointed out. 'I admit, it would have kept Kore's side of it under cover; was that what you had in mind? That I shouldn't know?'

'More what I hoped,' she admitted reluctantly. 'Oh, please, Arkady, you can't be too hard on her, surely? She didn't know, that's one thing I'm absolutely sure of. He sent her a print of the photograph to threaten her with.' She wrinkled her forehead. 'He wanted her to go to bed with him and she turned him down. He didn't realise how young she really is, I think. Girls often put a couple of years on their age when they're sixteen, they don't like to be thought of as children . . .'

'And . . .?' Arkady brought her back to the point.

'And she refused him—which I think shows she has a lot of sense. After that, he must have been holding that photograph over her head—she went very moody, didn't you notice?' Joanna stopped being apologetic and started to fight. 'You *should* have seen that; after all, she's your daughter!'

'A daughter who wasn't very kind to you when we were first married. I'm surprised you defend her.'

'We-ell,' Joanna tried to be fair, 'we were married in a bit of a rush and you sprang me on her out of the blue, so it couldn't have been easy for her. She couldn't have found it easy—having a brand new stepmother plonked on her lap whether she liked it or not.'

'We should have asked her permission!' Arkady snorted derisively. 'Perhaps that's the way you do things in England, but I'm not an Englishman. I'm Greek, and we do things differently.'

'Oh, I know all about that,' she grimaced. 'Head of the house—your word is law and all the rest of it, but she ought to have had some say or been given an opportunity to get to know me a bit.'

'At the time,' he told her blandly, 'I didn't notice any signs of hanging back on your part. You were as eager as I was, so why should I consider Kore when you obviously didn't?'

'Because I . . .' Joanna hesitated and hastily

rephrased 'loved you' into 'I wasn't thinking.' She glowered at him. 'Just remember, I was a free agent, I didn't have your problem. I had nobody to consider except myself and I suppose I didn't try as hard as I should have done. But this time I felt we might be getting somewhere—I don't expect her to love me, but I was hoping she'd trust me—and you've gone and ruined it, poking your nose in where you weren't wanted or needed!'

'You're only angry because I stepped in and spoiled your little triumph.' He spared a glance from the road to grin at her. 'St Joanna to the rescue—and what would you have done if he'd caught you in the act and used a few strong-arm tactics on you? You were trespassing, doing wanton damage to a man's property.'

'I would have kicked his shins and escaped.' Joanna thought about how hard she would have kicked, and smiled blissfully. This was one instance when violence would have been permissible and enjoyable!

'Stupid!' Arkady brought her out of her daydream and down to earth with a bump. 'You wouldn't have stood a chance—*and* you know it. You should be thanking me, not biting my head off. In any case, you are my woman, and no other man is going to touch you.' The Range Rover bumped over a pothole and lurched round a bend in the winding road, so for a few seconds he concentrated on the driving, but when they reached a straighter, smoother piece of road, he lifted one hand from the wheel and laid it on her knee. 'Now, be quiet, *agape*, until I get us home.'

'I've got permission to speak my mind when we arrive?'

'No,' he shook his head and the hand on her knee tightened. 'We will have lunch, then you will feed our son, and afterwards—we are going to be alone to get some things decided. Our present relationship is good, but it could be improved. Each time I touch you, you give the impression that I'm despoiling a virtuous woman—only for a short while, because you soon forget whatever it is that's spoiling that first few moments, but it's not as it was when we first married. That was perfection and I want it back. So I shall lock us in until everything is straight between us . . .'

'It might take a long time,' Joanna broke in jeeringly, 'maybe a week or maybe even for ever!'

'The longer, the better! We don't come out until I've found again the woman I married. No more talking now, we are about to arrive.'

There was a welcoming committee on the patio—Sylvie, still humping Dion around on her almost non-existent hip, and Kore, keeping well in the background. Joanna caught her stepdaughter's eye and gave a very slight nod. It didn't lighten Kore's air of gloom, but she visibly relaxed. Her eyes were a bit puffy still from weeping, and although Jo wanted to comfort her, assure her that her father had seen neither prints nor negatives and that she, Joanna, was going to be as discreet as a Swiss banker; one look at Arkady's forbidding face kept her silent.

Instead she raised her nose and sniffed at the aroma of one of Anna's variations on moussaka, asked Sylvie if Dion would wait for half an hour and went off to wash her hands before lunch. There was little time for thought, speed was of the essence, but Joanna found herself pausing with either the soap or the towel in her hands and staring blankly at nothing as she worried answers to hypothetical questions. She was determined not to get Kore into any more trouble. Enough was enough for one day!

Ilone came down to lunch, superbly dressed in a tailored linen skirt and shirt—all honey but with a sting behind the sweetness.

'You look quite animated,' she told Joanna. 'I think you are a person who needs stimulation. You find it dull here with only your family for company, *ne*?'

Joanna looked up glassily over a forkful of moussaka. 'No, I don't find it dull,' she said patiently but firmly and finally. 'Do you?' She had added the question to keep the conversation on the subject of dullness—she didn't want it skittering off to what she had been doing in Paleokastritsa. Kore was already looking better, less strained, and that was how Joanna wanted it, but she had let Ilone get hold of the conversational ball and when Ilone threw it, she scored a bullseye every time. She scored one now.

'You managed to settle the matter of that disgusting photograph taken of Kore?'

Joanna's 'Yes' was swamped by Arkady's 'Certainly! Which is as it should be, Ilone. I am her father and Joanna stands in place of a mother to my daughter. It was our duty and our pleasure.'

'You knew about it, Arkady?' The Greek woman's voice shook with chagrin.

'Kore told me,' he said flatly with a brief nod, and his smile glimmered at his daughter. 'Fortunately she had told Joanna first, so no time was wasted, and my wife is more competent to deal with such a problem than either you or I. Also she has a great deal of courage, and this, allied with what I can only describe as infernal impudence, did all that was necessary. Strictly speaking, there was no need for me to go there at all.' His fugitive smile, which so transformed his face, glimmered across the table at Joanna, almost teasingly, and she basked in the warmth of it, beginning to feel almost as courageous as he had said she was, although she knew herself for an arrant coward.

'When I arrived at the taverna,' he continued smoothly, 'everything had been done. The young man, fortunately, was not there.'

'You mean that Joanna went into a man's rooms uninvited?' Ilone seemed to be suffering from shock at the very thought, her face was a rigid mask of distaste, and Joanna's eyes sparkled with anger as she dropped her fork on to her plate and glared at the Greek woman.

'What offends you so much?' she demanded belligerently. 'That I went there uninvited or that I went there at all? Somebody had to do something...'

'Kore should have confessed to her father,' Ilone broke in waspishly. 'She should have done that at once.'

'Kore had nothing to confess!' Rage boiled up in Joanna so that she became uncaring. 'Unless Arkady would disapprove of her taking an early morning swim when the beach was deserted. We aren't living in the past!'

Ilone had the advantage, she wasn't losing *her* temper. 'In my opinion——' she began reasonably.

'I don't give a damn for your opinion!' Joanna broke in fiercely. 'I did what I thought was best and I got away with it—although,' she admitted, 'I'll confess to being a bit scared when Hank Sommers walked in unexpectedly.'

'You mean you were alone with him in his rooms?'

'Not a bit.' Joanna grinned at Kore while she answered Ilone's question. 'By that time your father had arrived, and he provided the muscle we needed to get out.'

'But what you did . . .' Ilone wasn't going to leave it alone, she was going to worry the subject to death, so Joanna stopped her before she could go any further.

'What I did,' she snapped, 'was done from the best of motives. Maybe it wasn't exactly ethical, but I don't give a damn about that. I was doing my best to protect Kore, and you have to admit that having her photograph in men's magazines all over the world—because that was what it would have meant. Yes,' as she caught Ilone's little sneer, 'that's what would have happened. From what I saw, Hank Sommers probably sells to the highest bidder, big and with a world-wide circulation—It wouldn't have been very nice, not for Kore and not for any of you. The fact that together Arkady and I were successful ought to excuse my methods.'

'You should have consulted Arkady first.' Ilone wasn't going to give up.

'So—I didn't. He wasn't here to consult, and all you could do, Ilone, was shout at Kore as if it was all her fault when it wasn't!'

'We have only your word for that,' the Greek woman bridled, and Joanna gave up.

'Not only my word but Kore's too—but you're

not going to believe either of us, are you? And I don't give a damn about that either. I can't understand you. Kore's some sort of relation, and yet you're willing—I could even say eager—to think the worst of her, but none of that matters now. It's done, and nothing you can say will change it. Right or wrong, I did it, and I'm not a bit ashamed. Everybody else seems to be quite happy—it's only you who's carping and criticising, and I can't see why.'

'A good point.' Arkady took it up and Joanna was grateful—she was a bit out of breath. 'Why, Ilone? Perhaps you'd explain.'

'Certainly.' Ilone breathed deeply through her nose so that the nostrils thinned, and qualified it. 'I will, if you think it necessary, but I've told you before, if you remember. I have nothing against Joanna except that her ways are not our ways ...'

'... and never will be!' Joanna laid down her fork, pushed back her chair and rose hastily. It was one thing to know one wasn't welcome to a certain member of the family, but another thing to hear it said aloud. She bit her tongue to prevent hot, angry words dropping from the end of it and became excessively polite and diplomatic. 'I really must go and see to Dion,' she muttered, and let her mouth curve into a bright, synthetic smile before she fled. But Arkady was quick to follow—it seemed she had no sooner shut the bedroom door behind her than he was opening it and coming in.

Sylvie hadn't brought the baby back yet, so they were alone in the room, and she swung round on him, her face stiff with anger and her eyes slitted.

'Don't you dare criticise my behaviour!' she

almost snarled. 'I think I behaved beautifully according to *my* standards, which I admit aren't yours.'

Arkady's magnificent scowl dissolved into a smile. 'Yes, you did, *gineka mou*—by any standards—but you disappointed both Kore and me. We were expecting an outburst, we were going to revel in it.' And as she looked stunned, 'A woman who was ready to take on Hank Sommers single-handed!—we expected something better than a muttered excuse followed by flight. I hope the flight stops here and doesn't continue back to London via the airport.'

'Leaving my baby here to be brought up by Ilone? Not on your sweet life!' snorted Joanna. 'The poor little thing would be a mass of repressions before it's six months old.' And only then did the full meaning of what he had said hit her and she gasped. 'You—you *wanted* a show-down?'

Arkady looked down at her consideringly. 'Don't you think we need one, Joanna, if we're ever to make a real success of our married life? And I've another question for you. Is my refusal to allow you to take Dion away with you the only reason you're staying here?'

'N-not altogether,' she mumbled as she turned away from him, only to be turned back—but oh, so gently. The anger had gone from her face, her eyes were no longer slitted but wide and a very clear grey between their thick fringing of sooty lashes. She raised them to Arkady's face, searching for something—some little clue which would tell her how to continue, but she could see nothing there, only a quiet waiting for the truth. It seemed at this moment that nothing else would do.

His eyes were very dark and Joanna felt as though she was drowning in them, and with a muffled gasp, she wrenched her own away.

'I'm waiting,' he reminded her.

'I know.' Her mouth felt dry and her tongue seemed too big for it. She gulped and licked her lips, deciding on a careless tone. If what she said was the wrong thing, she could always manufacture a careless laugh and tell him she was joking, of course!

'I—I still love you, which is silly of me, and sillier still to admit it aloud. It gives you such an advantage, if you see what I mean. I'm a woman and you're an attractive man and my husband to boot, so it's quite reasonable that I should want you. I thought I'd grown out of loving you, but I haven't.' She shrugged and ended up with her shoulders in a defeated droop. 'I didn't want you to know that,' she added sadly.

'But it's all I need to know.' Gently, Arkady reached out and took her hands in his own. 'I too thought you had only desire left and I would have to make the best I could of that—but it wasn't really enough, Joanna, not when I could remember how it had been.' The slow, steady pull of his hands brought her up against him so that beneath her cheek she could hear the steady throb of his heartbeat.

'*Agape mou,*' he said into her hair, his voice very soft and deep, 'I've been cruel to you, haven't I? But you must understand. I married you—a girl, untried and so much younger. I knew what I was doing, but after a while I began to ask myself if you had known what you were doing. I began to worry in case, once the novelty had worn off, you'd start to have second thoughts, and it seemed to me that was what was happening. When you ran away, I thought I would give you time. I didn't want a tearful reconciliation that wouldn't last—I wanted a fresh start.'

'Based on threats?' Joanna lifted her head and eyed him sardonically. 'That's a fine basis for a relationship, I must say!'

'It was the only way I had,' he pointed out. 'I knew you wouldn't be parted from the baby and it seemed a perfect chance to start all over again— better than reasoning with you, as I would have had to do if you hadn't had the child—and I didn't force you into anything else, remember? What has happened between us since you returned was with your full consent, and then,' he gave an odd little laugh of self-mockery, 'what did I find? Not that you were bored, that life here wasn't lively enough for you, but that you were riddled with jealousy and suspicion.'

'And why shouldn't I have been?' she demanded fiercely, a fierceness that diminished into a grumble. 'Who told you about that anyway? Ilone?'

'No, my silly little wife, not Ilone. You did, *agape*, when you accused me of having a lover. You said you saw me, remember?'

'And I did!' She leaned back against his arms to get a better view of his face. 'In the garden, you and Ilone. If I was wrong, why didn't you just say so?'

Arkady shrugged. 'In time, Joanna, we shall think alike, but we haven't reached that stage yet. I was angry that you should trust me so little, condemn me on such slight grounds. I didn't make allowances for your ignorance of our ways. Had I taken a mistress, she would certainly never have lived under the same roof as my daughter. I would have bought or built her a small house, at a convenient distance from here. But that you should think it, accuse me of it, gave me a little hope for the future. It could have been possessiveness, but you aren't a possessive person, my love.'

'You and she were kissing.' It still rankled, and Joanna dwelt on it. After all, it was better to be thought green with jealousy than to have Kore dumped into hot water again, almost before the girl was free of the first lot.

'You only guessed that.' Arkady pulled her back against him with a chuckle. 'It was much too dark for you to see clearly who was kissing whom.' He became serious. 'Are you going to stay this time, *karthia mou*, or do you still want to escape? We'll set our house in order, there will be just you and me, Kore and Dion—Ilone is going back to Athens. I'm grateful for what she has done, but it's time she started to live her own life. I shall find a husband for her, or better still, since she's wealthy enough to pick and choose, *we* will select one.'

Poor Ilone! For the first time, Joanna felt pity for the woman who loved her husband so well and so unwisely. He hadn't even noticed! And then she looked up into his face and called herself a fool. Of course Arkady had noticed, but she was now sure he had never done anything about it.

'Leave me out of it,' she snorted softly. 'I've got enough to do minding my own business.'

'Yes, you will,' he agreed almost smugly. 'I'm

going to provide you with plenty to do. You tend to start imagining things if you're idle.'

'And how are you going to do that?'

Arkady didn't answer at once. He cocked his head at the patter of Sylvie's little boots coming along the balcony and measured the time they had left to themselves. It was so little, and his kiss took up most of it. Joanna emerged from it shaken and flushed to hear his murmur in her ear just as Sylvie reached the long window that opened into the bedroom.

'I shall love you, *koritse*, and I shall keep you busy with always a baby at your breast and a toddler clinging to your skirts . . .'

Joanna stifled a gasp of outraged laughter as she struggled out of his arms and went to take her baby from a prim, efficient Sylvie. 'It sounds like a prison sentence,' she threw the words at him over her shoulder.

'That bad?' He gave Sylvie a smile and a dismissive nod, and when she had gone—'Shall you dislike it so much? We Greeks are very fond of children.'

'So am I, but in moderation.' Joanna hushed Dion's hunger cry and her eyes sparkled at her husband over the baby's head. 'Of course, if they're all like this one I shan't mind a bit, but when would we have any time to ourselves?'

Arkady put his arm round them both, drawing them close. 'They will be good babies, happy and contented,' he comforted her, then smiled. 'With them we shall share the days, but the nights, *koritse*—the nights will be ours alone!'

Coming Next Month in Harlequin Romances!

2731 TEARS OF GOLD Helen Conrad
The mystery man found panning for gold on a young woman's California estate sparks her imagination—especially when she learns he's bought her family home!

2732 LORD OF THE AIR Carol Gregor
There's turbulence ahead when the owner of a flying school wants to build a runway on his neighbor's land. He disturbs her privacy, not to mention her peace of mind.... .

2733 SPRING AT SEVENOAKS Miriam MacGregor
A young Englishwoman's visit to a New Zealand sheep station arouses the owner's suspicions. No woman could be counted on to live in such isolation! Why should she be any different?

2734 WEDNESDAY'S CHILD Leigh Michaels
Is it generosity that prompts a man to offer his estranged wife money for their son's medical expenses? Or is it a bid to get her under his thumb again?

2735 WHERE THE GODS DWELL Celia Scott
A fashion photographer abandons her glamorous career for an archaeological dig in Crete. But she has second thoughts when she falls in love...and clashes with old-world Greece.

2736 WILDERNESS BRIDE Gwen Westwood
Concern brings an estranged wife to her husband's side on an African wilderness reserve when blindness threatens him. But he insists on reconquering the wilderness...and her!

Here's how to get this special offer from Harlequin! As simple as 1...2...3!

1. Each month, save one Treasury Edition coupon from your favorite Romance or Presents novel.
2. In four months you'll have saved four Treasury Edition coupons (<u>only one coupon per month allowed</u>).
3. Then all you have to do is fill out and return the order form provided, along with the four Treasury Edition coupons required and $1.00 for postage and handling.

Mail to: Harlequin Reader Service

In the U.S.A.
2504 West Southern Ave.
Tempe, AZ 85282

In Canada
P.O. Box 2800, Postal Station A
5170 Yonge Street
Willowdale, Ont. M2N 6J3

RT1-D-2

Please send me my FREE copy of the Janet Dailey Treasury Edition. I have enclosed the four Treasury Edition coupons required and $1.00 for postage and handling along with this order form.

(Please Print)

NAME_____

ADDRESS_____

CITY_____

STATE/PROV._____ ZIP/POSTAL CODE_____

SIGNATURE_____

This offer is limited to one order per household.

SUPPLIES LIMITED

This special Janet Dailey offer expires January 1986.

H·A·R·L·E·Q·U·I·N

FIRST·CLASS
Sweepstakes

OFFICIAL RULES

1. NO PURCHASE NECESSARY. To enter, complete the official entry/order form. Be sure to indicate whether or not you wish to take advantage of our subscription offer.

2. Entry blanks have been preselected for the prizes offered. Your response will be checked to see if you are a winner. In the event that these preselected responses are not claimed, a random drawing will be held from all entries received to award not less than $150,000 in prizes. This is in addition to any free, surprise or mystery gifts which might be offered. Versions of this sweepstakes with different prizes will appear in Preview Service Mailings by Harlequin Books and their affiliates. Winners selected will receive the prize offered in their sweepstakes brochure.

3. This promotion is being conducted under the supervision of Marden-Kane, an independent judging organization. By entering the sweepstakes, each entrant accepts and agrees to be bound by these rules and the decisions of the judges, which shall be final and binding. Odds of winning in the random drawing are dependent upon the total number of entries received. Taxes, if any, are the sole responsibility of the prize winners. Prizes are nontransferable. All entries must be received by August 31, 1986.

4. The following prizes will be awarded:

   (1) Grand Prize: Rolls-Royce™ *or* $100,000 Cash!
   (Rolls-Royce being offered by permission of Rolls-Royce Motors Inc.)

   (1) Second Prize: A trip for two to Paris for 7 days/6 nights. Trip includes air transportation on the Concorde, hotel accommodations...PLUS...$5,000 spending money!

   (1) Third Prize: A luxurious Mink Coat!

5. This offer is open to residents of the U.S. and Canada, 18 years or older, except employees of Harlequin Books, its affiliates, subsidiaries, Marden-Kane and all other agencies and persons connected with conducting this sweepstakes. All Federal, State and local laws apply. Void in the province of Quebec and wherever prohibited or restricted by law. Winners will be notified by mail and may be required to execute an affidavit of eligibility and release, which must be returned within 14 days after notification. Canadian winners will be required to answer a skill-testing question. Winners consent to the use of their name, photograph and/or likeness for advertising and publicity purposes in conjunction with this and similar promotions without additional compensation. One prize per family or household.

6. For a list of our most current prize winners, send a stamped, self-addressed envelope to: WINNERS LIST, c/o Marden-Kane, P.O. Box 10404, Long Island City, New York 11101

Take 4 books & a surprise gift FREE

Experience the warmth of . . .

Harlequin Romance

**The original romance novels.
Best-sellers for more than 30 years.**

Delightful and intriguing love stories
by the world's foremost writers
of romance fiction.

Be whisked away to dazzling
international capitals . . .
or quaint European villages.
Experience the joys of falling in love . . .
for the first time, the best time!

Harlequin Romance

**A uniquely absorbing journey
into a world of superb romance reading.**

Wherever paperback books are sold, or through
Harlequin Reader Service

In the U.S.
2504 West Southern Avenue
Tempe, AZ 85282

In Canada
P.O. Box 2800, Postal Station A
5170 Yonge Street
Willowdale, Ontario M2N 6J3

**No one touches the heart of a woman
quite like Harlequin!**

R-111